COMEUPPANCE

STORIES FROM THE 1960S

Michael C. Ahn

COMEUPPANCE
Stories from the 1960s

Copyright Michael C. Ahn, 2015

Some of the stories in this book have appeared in the following publications: "Mrs. Shelton" in *Lascaux Review*, "A Clean Slate" in *Paradise Review*, "The Fourth Chimp" in *The Vehicle Magazine*, and "Sailors Take Warning" in *Poydras Review*.

Vineyard Books
836 Anacapa St, #974
Santa Barbara, CA 93102

ISBN 978-0-692-36593-9

Cover design by Michael C. Ahn

Manufactured in the United States of America
First printing January 2015

To Suzanne

CONTENTS

MRS. SHELTON

SEEING HER ALLURE was like discovering a beautiful nun shrouded in heavy habit. She kept her glasses on even though she didn't need them for driving, and her honey brown hair was wound in a swirl, strands escaping as if she'd just gotten out of bed. Her figure had not changed much since her college years—still slim, but with a fullness that separated her from the girls. When she walked the hallways, she clutched books against her chest. The boys didn't bring her up in locker room talks as they did the younger teachers.

In 1962 Franklin High had hired Elizabeth Shelton to teach English with a one-year contract and an option to extend. I learned later her husband was a Navy captain stationed in Norfolk some twenty miles away, and as a matter of Navy practice, he was relocated every two years. By age 32 she had taught English at American schools on military bases in Hawaii, Guam, and Japan.

On the first day of Mrs. Shelton's class, I studied her face and heard little of what she had to say. She had no makeup, not even powder. Her lips were swollen red, the upper lip larger than the lower, and her wide eyebrows weren't plucked; her black pupils contrasted with her pale blue eyes. Though she didn't sit like the other teachers or hide behind a podium, she moved little as she stood in front of the class. I watched her every gesture, only listening to her words when I studied her inflections. When she looked my way, I'd quickly look down to my desk thinking I'd be unnoticed. A month into the semester I knew Mrs. Shelton's favorite dress and color.

With few friends I was probably labeled a loner, my reflective nature obvious to others—maybe because I was never without a book. I read before morning classes, during lunch, and sometimes in class. Even in grade school I had learned to fake attention to the teacher with a book balanced on my lap. I liked people but I was most comfortable with myself.

The Scarlet Letter was the first assignment in Mrs. Shelton's class. She talked casually of Hester Prynne's adultery and sin. Back then, such things weren't discussed in Tidewater country, in or out of class, especially by a woman. She spent a week on the book, and I was hooked by her discussions. I was not always at ease in class, but I looked forward to the assigned essays and papers where I could try out my literary insights. She wrote little praises on the backs of my papers, which I guarded like secret notes between friends.

Even on weekends Mrs. Shelton wouldn't leave my head. I thought of her on the bus, at my desk, and in my bed. I suspected my mother noticed me at times, gazing at or playing with my food. I'd had crushes before but this was different. She was older and married, but she consumed me fully. At times I felt as if I were a chess piece, sitting on a square with a finite number of moves that led to nowhere.

Spring came early that year, the azaleas blooming before Easter vacation. I landed a job in the library shelving books, perfunctory tasks taking a small portion of my last period. One March day I looked out the library window and sighted Mrs. Shelton sitting on the steps to the football field. She was marking papers with her ballpoint pen, inattentively repositioning her hair. I stood motionless and stared, bothered by perspiration under my collar. I knew I'd go to her, but like a deer hesitating before taking steps to a pond, I lingered.

"Mrs. Shelton," I said.

"Thomas," she said, looking up. She scanned the unclouded sky. "The sun is wonderful. Have you been workng in the library? Sit down."

I thought she must have noticed me in the library. I asked her assignment questions and she was more than polite; I was sure she welcomed my company.

Days drew out as I waited for my last class period, waiting to see if she would be sitting on the steps. When rain fell, I solaced myself with thoughts of her next class. On other days I waited by the window, careful to join her infrequently, not to risk her not coming out at all. When I left my duties to talk to her, I had ready a clever excuse.

By May Mrs. Shelton spent little time in the faculty lounge, preferring her free period outside the library steps. I imagined she even anticipated me, but I was cautious and spread out my visits. On the days I refrained, I shielded myself in the stacks and watched her as if she were my favorite character in a staged play.

"I wish you were going to college in the fall," she chided me one day. "You're uncommonly intelligent, Thomas."

Sitting next to her, I caught a faint whiff of her cologne or maybe bath oil. I stole a glance of her cotton skirt, of the outlines of her thighs. My breathing elevated, I inhaled deeply to slow its tempo. A yellow butterfly floated by.

"Well, I've already signed up for the Army. I'll be heading out to Fort Bragg for basic training two weeks after school," I said with some pride. "Besides, there's no money. Miss Gregory told me the G.I. Bill should help once I get out."

That past fall I had talked to Miss Gregory, the guidance counselor, a former gym teacher who had been promoted to a desk job when her obesity prevented her from her duties. She wasn't very knowledgeable or encouraging, but she touted the advantages of a military career, with no mention of SATs, scholarships or other academic options.

"Thomas, there are funds for students like you now," Mrs. Shelton persisted. "There are government scholarships and grants, especially from the major schools. I wish we had talked earlier in the year."

"Well, maybe after the Army," I said.

"Please promise me you'll take the college boards next year. I think you're gifted, Thomas. Would you consider studying English, or literature?"

I had not given thought to college. The few and the wealthy ended up at the University of Virginia or William and Mary, and others went to teachers colleges. But the majority of students left school for jobs at local retail stores, construction work, gas stations, or the military. Before I left school, Mrs. Shelton had agreed to extend her contract another year, and I promised her I would write.

IN THE SUMMER of '63 the war in Vietnam wasn't front page news. The nation started to take notice of the civil rights marches, waited in line to see *Dr. No*, and listened to Jan and Dean. After basic training, soldiers were sent to Germany, Korea, Japan, and other parts of the world, but I was assigned to the 9th Logistic Command, part of MAAG—Military

Assistance and Advisory Group in Vietnam; the Army placed me in their motor pool in Saigon. At the time Americans were in an advisory role, there were few casualties, and the war was still limited for GI's. If I were to create a job for myself, I couldn't have done better. I wasn't required to carry a gun, march, or stand guard duty. At eighteen I supervised a dozen Vietnamese who were skilled mechanics, some of whom were old enough to have been my father.

I sat at a gray steel desk, handing out work orders, tracking schedules, and writing weekly reports. My only supervisor was a Sergeant Stickles, a beefy semi-literate from Georgia who was glad to have me doing all his work. Stickles told me, "Hanson, I'm a firm believer in keeping my desk without no papers. And your ass is to make sure of that. Hear?" And then he'd slip off.

The Vietnamese motor pool workers were men, save one—Luong Tuyen. She spoke French but she had also picked up English from her father, an accountant who had worked for an Australian trading company. As a childless widow who supported her mother, she was grateful for the job with the Americans.

Tuyen became more of a mentor than an assistant to me, guiding me in weaving through the bureaucracy, ordering equipment, and dealing with worker problems. She even showed me how to handle irate colonels demanding unscheduled drivers. "Toma," she would call me as a Frenchwoman would. "Never say no to lieutenant colonel. Say yes. Always. Then we figure something out. Sometimes we just forget. Then say yes again. Better that way."

I liked her wit and sarcasm, which was more American than Asian. She was tall for a Vietnamese, delicate and thin, unlike the more curved American women. Her straight black hair was permed at the ends, mimicking Western styles, and her facial features were subdued. Her Oriental eyes were more triangular shaped than other Vietnamese, imparting a look of sadness. She had an unclear smile fixed on the corners of her mouth.

I was sure Tuyen liked me also. Once during a break she told me she was glad I worked in the office and that I was like a waft of fresh air, different than the other soldiers who were affable but just plain slow. A year and a half after my arrival, she invited me for a Vietnamese dinner at her house, and for the next six months we became secret lovers. At first my callow flesh insisted urgent and immediate satisfaction, often leaving her exhausted and silently unsatisfied. And again she became my teacher. "Toma, woman satisfaction more important to *you* than your satisfaction," she said with her Vietnamese accent. Another inscrutable aphorism, I thought, but I eventually got it. She guided me—my tempo, cadence. I saw her tensely wound body spasmodic then limp, and for days the feelings lingered, a quiet satisfaction. I hardly remembered my own.

I saw Tuyen on weekends and even during work days. She lived on a street wide enough for a couple of bicycles, more like an alley, crisscrossing like paths in an ant farm. Saigon was replete with such backstreets, crowds flowing through day and night with nonstop commerce and commotion and the pervasive aroma of strange spices and the stench of open sewage. And I didn't feel conspicuous among American GIs roaming the winding passages covered with strip bars and street walkers. Though she never left my thoughts, Mrs. Shelton was ten thousand miles away. Tuyen was with me now, but we both understood our affair would not be permanent.

I wrote Mrs. Shelton three times during my first year in Vietnam, and she responded promptly, asking me questions of my Army life, the war, and the Orient; and she didn't fail to remind me about college applications. The following spring she wrote that she had agreed to another year with the school. Her husband was to be assigned to Subic Bay in the Philippines in February, and she would finish out her teaching year and join him afterwards.

I took the SATs offered on the army base and applied to colleges in Virginia and New York. In April the APO (Army Post Office) delivered a couple of thick packets in Saigon which began: "We are pleased..." And as Mrs. Shelton had predicted, financial packages were also included. When she opened my letter that spring, she immediately wrote back how wonderful the news was, how proud she was, and how I would love college. She also wanted to see me before she left for the Philippines in June.

I HAD LEFT Virginia almost two years ago. In her last letter Mrs. Shelton had given me her number and told me to call her as soon as I arrived. The bus depot had one pay phone, and I was relieved when I heard a dial tone. When she answered, I swallowed to wet my throat.

"Wait at the depot, I'll be there in twenty minutes," she said.

Her voice hadn't changed, and her image became clearer to me as I pictured her lips pucker as they sometimes did before talking.

I sat outside on an old wooden bench. Two Negro gentlemen sat across from me, smoking and chitchatting about their connection. The late afternoon sun began to lose its strength and I considered calling my mother, but she would have to wait; besides, no one knew my schedule.

A beige '61 AMC Rambler drove up to the curve and Mrs. Shelton stepped out. She wasn't wearing her glasses. "Thomas!" she called.

I was about to say Mrs. Shelton, but I caught myself. "Hello, Elizabeth," I said as I picked up my duffle bag and moved towards her. She held both of my upper arms and kissed me on my cheek.

The last time I'd seen her on the library steps, my heart pounded just being near her; this time it raced but the school boy anxiety was gone. She had driven twenty miles to see me, I thought, maybe she looked a little older than I remembered though she was still beautiful. No, she hadn't changed much, but I realized perhaps I had. I eyed her movements as she walked on her high heels to her car.

"Have you eaten, Thomas? You must be hungry," she said,

putting her car into gear.

I inhaled her scent, arousing feelings from the past. The car windows were down on Highway 58, and I felt the twilight air, still humid and warm. The pastures with unending fences seemed foreign, and I could make out farm animals moving aimlessly. The Virginia countryside was so vast, I thought—I had forgotten. I smelled cut grass and wild onions, memories of my youth dashed through me, and I took a deep breath. It was good to be on an American highway, but I thought it was even better sitting next to Elizabeth.

"You've changed, Thomas, you've filled out a bit," she said smiling. "You move differently, slower." She paused. "Well, we better get you some food. There's a good Italian restaurant in my neighborhood."

Elizabeth did most of the talking in the car. She asked all the expected questions of Army life, the fighting, and college plans. I wanted to ask about her husband, but I didn't. There was little I knew about her: Why were there no children? What was she doing married to a military man—a Navy captain obviously much older than she. It seemed to me she should be married to a college professor or a lawyer. But I was glad to be with her and had difficulty subduing myself.

"We're fortunate in our timing," she said. "I have to take this car to the pier tomorrow to be shipped to the Philippines. The apartment is in shambles, everything is boxed up. All paid by the Navy, thank goodness."

"You'll be taking off the day after tomorrow?" I asked.

"Believe it or not, I've done everything I am supposed to.

I've closed my bank account, gotten my passport, finished the Navy paperwork, filled out the change of address at the post office... everything. I do have to take the car to the pier. They'll come in the morning and move everything in the apartment. Then, all I have to do is get myself to Dulles Airport with couple of suitcases."

"I guess I just made it," I said. "I mean, a day later and I wouldn't have been able to see you."

"We're almost there," she said, turning off the highway.

I watched her lips move. It was painful.

"You'll like Gino," she continued. "There are not many Italian restaurants here. In fact I think it was the first Italian restaurant in Norfolk. I hope you like Italian."

The restaurant was full and Elizabeth was right. It was comfy, with red-checkered tablecloths and candles stuck in old wine bottles. I smelled garlic.

"Elizabeth!" Gino yelled out. "How's the captain, have you heard from him?"

"Good evening, Gino. I received a letter just a few days ago." She introduced him to me as one of her students who'd just come back from an Army tour. Elizabeth asked for a glass of house Chianti, salad, and veal; I had never heard of veal. I ordered the only Italian dish I knew—spaghetti and meat-balls. I wasn't a drinker, probably the only one in his bar-racks back in Saigon.

Elizabeth could not hear enough of my stories, occasionally breaking her attention to sip the Chianti. Her attention pleased me, and I narrated my life in the Orient like a journalist returning from an assignment: the tense political state, the coming war, the confused countryside, bizarre customs, steamy city backstreets, the people. I did mention Tuyen, but not our relationship.

The single candle flickered as I sat across from her, and I was unaware of the blurred chatter of others in the room. Our eyes met regularly during the evening, and I thought Elizabeth looked away as if to conceal her feelings. I was sure I was right.

Gino approached us. "How about some dessert, Elizabeth? We have your favorite spumoni."

"Thomas, would you like one? Smooth Italian ice cream with nuts and fruit."

"No, I'm full."

"No, Gino. But I'll have just one more Chianti," she said.

She'd already had two, I thought, and I began to think I might be sleeping at Elizabeth's tonight. Maybe. Where else at this time of night? She wasn't going to drive me anywhere in her condition.

At 10:30 Gino and his help began their close-up routine. Elizabeth turned to Gino, raised her finger and silently mouthed for the check.

"No, Elizabeth, the dinner is on the house," Gino said. "We won't be seeing you for a while."

She stood up, and after their "please write" and "I'll see you when I return," she thanked Gino and kissed him on the cheeks. Elizabeth told me it was late, and she may have drunk more Chianti than she should have. Then she offered me her living room couch for the night, quite matter-of-factly. She would drive me to the bus depot in the morning.

The apartment complex had quadruplex units, Virginia red clay bricks and white window frames with Jeffersonian touches. The humid night air was still, except for crickets chirping.

"Ok, we're home," she said and turned the keys to kill the engine. No other words were spoken. She led me up the stairs and I followed with my eyes fixed on Elizabeth's back. When she unlocked the door, a single floor lamp lit the living room—bare walls, strewn moving-cartons, and scattered furniture everywhere. I smelled fresh cardboard boxes. She took several steps into her apartment, turned and held out her hand. She led me through the short hallway to her dark bedroom, and passing the room's light switch, walked towards the nightstand. I stood by the door.

Fragments of light passed into the bedroom through the Venetian blinds, and with the living room light sneaking in from the hallway, I could make out her eyes looking at me. In silence Elizabeth unbuttoned her cream-colored blouse, and without pausing, unhooked her brassiere. Her pear-shaped breasts were disproportionate to her narrow shoulders, the tips proudly pointing to the ceiling like forsythia buds in April. Her skirt dropped to the floor.

I stepped toward her. I unbuttoned my shirt and bent over to slip my legs out of my khakis as she stared at me. Before straightening my back, I gently kissed her stomach. Holding my head with both hands, Elizabeth let out a sigh. I rose to

13

take her lips.

THE ROOM WAS muggy, the smell of two bodies sweltering in ceaseless flux—the windows opaque, condensed frenzy. Echoes of our intensity reverberated in the room and our breathing slowed. Elizabeth's left arm was wrapped around my neck while I faced down on my stomach, and within minutes she fell into a deep sleep. I laid motionless—tracks of perspiration rolled down my back like raindrops skidding down a window pane. The electric clock showed midnight, the long hand droning. I looked at the beautiful woman lying beside me.

When I opened my eyes, I was alone in the bare room, mourning doves calling outside the windows. I moved slowly off the bed to pick up my pants lying on the floor. Elizabeth? I walked to the bathroom in the hallway and relieved myself. I lowered my head to the running faucet and gulped to quench my dried mouth, and then I dashed my face with the water and grabbed a towel from the rack. When I wandered into the living room, skirting the mountain of boxes, the front door opened.

"Oh, good morning, Thomas," she said.

"Morning."

"I ran out to the 7-11 to get some coffee and glazed do-nuts. My kitchen is totally bare."

Sipping my coffee, I looked at her, searching, and she returned a smile.

"Thomas, the movers will be here early, in about an hour.

I'll have to be here, so I'm afraid we should move along to the bus station soon."

I'd expected her to mention the previous night, or our new consonance. But there was no discussion.

"Sure. That would be fine," I said, "You've got a lot to do."

During the fifteen-minute ride to the bus station, she talked of her memories of college, her education, and the happiness she felt for the coming changes in my life. There was no mention of exchanging mailing addresses.

As the Rambler slowed to the curb in front of the terminal, she put the gear into park. She reached for the glove compartment and removed a wrapped box. "For your trip," she said, placing it in my hands. Then she said softly, "Thomas, you are an unusual young man. You'll make some woman very happy." She then leaned towards me and touched my cheek.

"Good bye, Elizabeth," I heard my voice say. I lifted my duffle bag from the back seat, looked at her once more, and walked toward the depot.

The parting was somber, I thought, an empty closure. The Greyhound bus smelled of cigarettes, and I took a seat in the back, looking once more out the tinted window. She had already disappeared but her last words lingered. I examined her gift—a book, I guessed, and tore off the wrapping. A gilded leather-bound copy of *Look Homeward, Angel* by Thomas Wolfe. She had probably recouped it from a box in her living room, I thought. A handwritten card was placed in the book, a note telling me to move on: "We have our fixed paths/ Look forward dearest Thomas/ A summerly life." It wasn't much of a consolation, I thought, but still she had signed it, "Love Elizabeth."

STILL IN BED I stared at the roving black spider on the pockmarked wall. My throat smarted as I turned my groggy head to the unmade bed across the room and smelled my new roommate's stale cigarettes in an ashtray on the floor. Muffled voices penetrated the door. My alarm clock hummed—I thought I'd turned it on but wasn't sure. The dorms, I was in Baker Hall. A familiar discomfort nagged me. I thought of Elizabeth, my eyes scanning the ceiling. Elizabeth.

I considered smacking the spider, splattering its innards on the wall, but instead decided to get up from my bed. I sat in front of my desk and reached for a half–drunk Coke, fizzless and warm. The gilded covers of Thomas Wolfe's book glistened, a corner of the note card visible; Wolfe was one of Elizabeth's favorites. I had brought the book with me but had not opened it. I pulled out the card and stared again at her cursive writing from a fountain pen:

> *June 3, 1965*
> *We have our fixed paths*
> *Look forward dearest Thomas*
> *A summerly life*
> *Love Elizabeth*

I had not understood the poem on the bus, but now I

thought that she might have meant our moments will always be part of my life. So the meaning was in the Haiku—a last secret note between friends.

A CLEAN SLATE

WHEN I TOLD my shrink I was leaving the city for Cornell in the Finger Lakes area, he talked about a milestone and key psychoanalytic juncture and all that psycho-jargon bull.

"It'll be a new beginning, Robert," he said. "A clean slate."

He was probably glad to get rid of me.

My parents have had me in analysis since '61 when I was thirteen, and I'm not sure what it has done for me. On the one hand, it's possible his sessions have taken a little load off them, because they were certain something wasn't quite right with me; but on the other hand, I don't think I have problems, nothing serious anyway. True, I don't connect well with people, but then most people aren't worth my time.

Dr. Gannon throws out words like "borderline personality disorder" and "dysfunctional schemata." He's one of those Park Avenue types with degrees from Hopkins and Harvard that charges $50 an hour. Over the last few years, maybe he's helped me figure out people. The only problem with me may be that I'm a genius. My IQ is off the charts, and getting a 1600 on my SATs was a breeze. The Wechsler Intelligence and the Stanford-Binet have placed me in the exceptional category.

When I was twelve, I was in a summer program for gifted children. It was funded by a foundation, Ford or Kaiser or something. On the first day they gathered the kids, about twenty of us, into a gymnasium. Then they gave each of us one clean sheet of paper, eight and a half by eleven.

"Okay children," the head teacher said. "We want you to make an airplane with the paper, a plane that will travel far. Whoever comes up with a design that travels the farthest will be the winner. And you've got five minutes."

I'm thinking, what's this supposed to prove? Anyway, all the kids wanted to show that they were a whiz. They were pathetic, tense and all consumed. I'll admit a few of the kids crafted prodigious designs, shapes and forms I'd had never seen. One kid folded his paper into a perfect missile—

symmetric and balanced, with little fan-like rudders. I crumpled my paper into a ball, wadded tight, and com-pressed.

When the five minutes were up, the teacher had us take turns, one at a time, to throw our planes. It was no contest. My wadded ball carried across the gym and then rolled to the wall. The teachers huddled in a spirited discussion and then their leader announced, "Robert Caldwell is the winner. His extraordinary design demonstrated uncommon creativity—a true genius."

I thought I was just bored.

The summer was filled with tedious classes, trig for sixth graders and pre-calc Boolean Logic. I don't remember whether the classes were the real stuff, it was too easy. On the last day of the summer program, we had a party with cupcakes and A&W root beer. At the time handwriting analysis was becoming a vogue and taken seriously, and it was supposed to reveal your intelligence and even your temperament. The teacher had everyone complete a handwriting summary of their experience in the program.

Again I was a step ahead of the game. When I'd heard about the handwriting theory in fourth grade, I began to mimic pen scripts of a genius—small, upright without slant, and the letter "e" that looked like an ampersand. Along with other traits, I continued to write like a genius since then. So, when the teachers examined my writing, they declared me to be a genius.

In grade school my parents bragged about me to all their

friends—how I received the highest scores on standardized tests, how I knew the names of every dinosaur from Brachyceratops to Triceratops by age three, how I had memorized every bird in the Peterson's bird book before I could read. But when I turned thirteen, they began to be concerned. It was June and my hobby was dragonflies, those insects that prey on mosquitoes and other bugs, but use flying mechanics like no other creature. They fly with four wings with unusual pitching strokes, up and down instead of back and forth. This allows them to hover like a helicopter and even shift into reverse. At rest they don't fold their wings like other insects but extend them horizontally as if to display their elegance.

I had about a dozen dragonflies in an empty fish bowl, fluttering and covered by a tin cap punched with holes. On my desk I would take them out, one at a time, and pluck their wings. I saw that they didn't die immediately but crawled aberrantly as if they were intoxicated. Within an hour or two, the plucked insects would cease to move. I wondered: Did they die from physical trauma or something else? I continued the experiment with several more and received the same results. I told my mother what I had done. She was horrified.

"What you did was cruel, Robert," she told me. "You shouldn't torture God's helpless creatures."

Her words only inspired me. I obtained a large cotton ball, lit it with a match, and dropped it into the fish bowl with the remaining dragonflies. For this experiment I closed the bowl with a cap without holes. The bluish smoke rose to the top of the bowl, slowly at first, then as the cotton turned black, the smoke thickened and became opaque. The dragonflies fought for positions at the top of the bowl, their wings fluttering as if on fire. One by one they dropped to the bottom, shivering briefly and then motionless.

Around this time my mother uncovered dirty magazines in my room—Betty Paige glossies showing Betty tied up to bedposts or holding a whip over a blindfolded guy. I bought them from this kid in the neighborhood who had stolen them from his father; I paid a bundle. My mother seized them but it was easy to get more.

My mother was troubled I didn't have friends. I had begun to play chess and had rapidly advanced to the master level by the time I joined the Manhattan Chess Club, where I spent my free hours. My mother was distressed that I would spend so many hours with old men staring at a chess board, and I'm sure she was also thinking that there weren't any teen girls around. But chess is a compelling game. Dr. Gannon knew a little about chess, and being a partial Freudian, he told me it was a game of patricide. Fifty bucks an hour, and that's what he had to tell me about the game. The queen, or the mother figure, was the most powerful, and the king was the weakest, though the most valuable. Two men stare at the same board for hours, not allowed to touch the opponent's pieces—conflicts surrounding aggression, homosexuality, masturbation and narcissism. That's how a psychiatrist and chess master named Reuben Fine explained it, so Gannon told me.

Aside from chess, physics devoured most of my time. I

started off with Newtonian physics and progressed to relativity. I had learned calculus by ninth grade, and from there physics was just a matter of reading the books and journals. Since starting high school I had won several science contests, a couple of them at the state level.

I learned of Hans Bethe from the American Institute of Physics Journal, which described his Nobel Prize for work in quantum electrodynamics in addition to his work on the atom bomb. But what impressed me was that he nurtured his protégé, Richard Feynman, who ended up receiving a Nobel Prize as well. So, I was willing to let Hans Bethe help me become the greatest physicist since Einstein and the first Nobel Laureate in my family history.

I was accepted at every college I applied to, along with some I hadn't applied to, and they all gave me scholarships. I considered Columbia and MIT, but my family encouraged me to go to a school in the countryside, away from the city.

My parents said they would drive me the 250 miles from the city, but I didn't want an escort; it seemed so puerile. They offered to fly me up on Mohawk Air from LaGuardia, but I don't like to fly. I don't trust airplanes, and I trust pilots even less. The train services had recently stopped, so I took a Greyhound. It wasn't bad. I had my physics books and dirty magazines to keep me company for the five-hour ride.

My parents also insisted I live in the dorms and have a roommate. They thought the dorm atmosphere would help me. Frankly, I disliked the idea of sharing a little room with someone else, but even Gannon supported the idea. "A roommate will help you to interact and socialize better," he had told me.

The minute I met my new roommate, I didn't like him. He sat at his desk in a blue shirt with a bow-tie. A bow-tie.

He jumped up. "Hi, Robert. I'm Alvin Holmes from Baaston." Baaston. He apologized for already having chosen his bed and desk. What did I care, they were both the same. Then he spittled our little room with small talk: what was my major, where in the city had I lived, what prep school had I attended, on and on. He was trying to be pleasant but I was bored.

Our dorm was at the bottom of a long hill leading to the main campus. It was built after the war, and the boxy architecture clashed with the rest of the campus like a polka dot tie over a Madras plaid shirt—like Alvin and me. I wished I had a room to myself and didn't know how long I would be able to last with this guy.

By the time I unloaded my suitcases and piled my books on my desk, the halls had filled with students and parents. The corridor echoed with hi-I'm-so-and-so small talk and chit chat, the wall phone ringing endlessly. It was hard to breathe. I excused myself from Alvin and set out to take a self-guided tour of campus.

There were towering elm trees all over the campus, and I admit they were striking, even more so than the ones in Central Park. I walked through the libraries and the student union building. I checked out the coeds, some who could have stepped out of *The Great Gatsby* carrying tennis rackets and wearing white headbands, and others swaggering like bull dykes. Women—that's another concern my parents had about me. I was an only child; they had placed all their eggs in one basket. And since they had never seen me with a girl, they were anxious. Dr. Gannon had prodded me about that once. I told him I wasn't a homo and that the whole idea of two men together was disgusting. But I also told to him that women were weak and inferior. How many Nobel winners in physics were women? Only one, Madame Curie. She had won in chemistry and physics, but it was really chemistry. There weren't any female grandmasters in chess either.

In the physics building I found Hans Bethe's office. The door was open, but he wasn't in. The office had books on shelves, a walnut desk, and reams of papers scattered everywhere. It was so ordinary. Maybe people aren't like objects in motion, I thought, predictable like equations.

As I continued my walk, I had difficulty imagining that ice a mile thick had covered all this land 10,000 years before. When the glaciers moved, inches at a time, the Finger Lakes were scratched out, and gorges that fed the lakes were created. One of those lakes and gorges bisected the campus. I stood on a bridge connecting the divide that separated the women's dorms from the rest of the university. Two hundred feet below, tiny specks of students swam and bathed beneath the falls. Some were jumping off the shale ledges, while others picnicked and drank beer and wine from gallon jugs. I could never fit in with these people, I thought. I have too much to do.

Loud music blared from some fraternity houses while others had live bands on their lawn. You could see brawny guys in T-shirts rolling kegs of beer into the houses, while their frat brothers cruised the campus roads in their convertibles, the racket grating my nerves.

A ten acre lake along a narrow strip of woods fed the gorge. The timbers stood tall at the edge of the water. I followed a dirt path, tree-covered, dark and cool. A mosquito buzzed around me and began to suck through the perspiration puddled on my neck. I slapped it dead and wiped my palm of smeared blood onto my pants. Suddenly I was mindful of the silence, the campus sounds buffered. I looked up at the sky, studying the rays of light piercing through branches in vibrating shafts. Lower down, the beams trembled off what appeared to be a vertical line against tangled branches. My eyes locked on to the pendulum tied to a large tree branch, a long rope with a man hanging at its end, his feet dangling above the ground. I froze. The body was motionless, like a heavy brass plumb pointing straight to the center of earth. I had once seen a dead dog in Central Park, but there was no comparison. As the shock tapered, I stepped closer to the lifeless body.

The man appeared too old to be a student, perhaps a young professor. He was dark-skinned and stout and wore a striped shirt. Maybe an East Indian or an Arab. His head fell limply to one side, and his swollen tongue protruded from his mouth, probably forced out by the noose pushing against the larynx. I had studied the signs of death years back when I had dismantled dragonflies. The man's tongue had turned red-black. I walked closer and twirled the body sideways, where I could see neck burns and brown scraped skin. His face and neck had darkened purple, with his jugular veins scrunched. The dried sheeny mucus pouring from his nose glistened, and his eyes were open wide, staring past me. A dark spot spread from the seat of his khakis, and I could smell the reek.

The man's hands were tied behind his back, the rope formed into large loops like bows. His hands weren't bound together but separated by several inches of rope. He was five feet off the ground, which meant that the weight of his falling body must have crushed the cervical spine. It must have been like the snap of a light switch, and I guessed that he didn't suffer in the final seconds. Not that it mattered.

I slogged out of the woods to the lodge next to the lake and asked an acne-faced kid behind the counter for his supervisor. He said no one was around. When I told him about the hanging, he turned white and told me I could call the campus police using the pay phone; he handed me a dime from the cash register. It wasn't long before three campus police cars arrived. I led them to the corpse, and then they called in the town police. A policeman questioned me, taking notes. Students began to make their way toward the commotion, but the cops turned them all back. It was doubtful that anyone but me and the authorities had witnessed the body. I was exhausted.

Later that day, the police interviewed me again back at my

dorm. A representative from the International Student Organization came with them. After the police departed he told me about the victim.

"His name was Kasuri, a Pakistani. He had just completed his doctorate in engineering. It will be ruled a suicide. That happens around here, but they usually jump into the gorge from one of the bridges. The police said this guy actually tied his hands in front of him and then managed to put his legs over them. He must have wanted to make sure he didn't try to free himself once he jumped from the branch."

"Okay, but why did he do it?"

"He had been living with an American girl. Kasuri's friends told us he had been despondent about going back to his wife in Rangpur. They say he was in love with his girlfriend here."

I didn't know much about love, but that didn't make sense to me. He had a wife in Pakistan and a new lover in America. Why not just leave your wife—she's on the other side of the world. Why kill yourself? I didn't get it. So I asked him. "And that was it? That was why he killed himself?"

"I'm sure it's more than that. I don't know Pakistani culture very well or his relationship with his wife and family. I'm told that his home in Pakistan didn't have indoor plumbing or running water. I don't know what was on his mind. His girlfriend doesn't want to talk about it."

I wished Dr. Gannon had been there. He'd have figured things out. Or at least he would have had a different language to describe what had taken place. To me it looked like this guy Kasuri could have had a new beginning in America. He had a clean slate. But maybe he didn't. He had a wife and family back home; maybe there were reasons he had to return to the life he had started with.

But me? I'm an American. I was raised with the shouts in the westerns. "Go west, young man. Go west." Go over the next hill and you have a new start. Just unhitch your old baggage. Maybe that's why Kasuri messed up. Maybe he didn't know what a clean slate was.

COMEUPPANCE

MY ROOMMATE HAD begged me to do him a favor—at the risk of lousing up my date, a guaranteed score—and I agreed. Why? Was it because I'm a good person? I don't think so, though frankly I can't think of any other reason.

One late September day in 1965 I was walking to my design studio, mulling over a spatial problem. Students were scattered on the Quad taking in the sun, a transistor radio softly playing the latest Beatles songs. Some were lying on the cool grass with their eyes closed, others sitting up and smoking their cigarettes like all was right with the world. After all, they still had time—months, or even years—before they had to catch a train to work, meet a mortgage, or pay dental bills.

The dome that crowned the Architecture School, my home away from my dorm, loomed ahead of me. I went to classes there, studied there, ate there, even slept there—I only went back to the dorm to shower and sleep. Architecture students had it worse than med students.

I was lost deep in my thoughts when I sighted a lone coed in a yellow blouse reading. She was seated on the grass, both her bare feet flat on the ground, knees pointing to the cloud-strewn sky. Completely still, she looked like a marble statue.

A breeze caught strands of her hazelnut hair. I shifted directions and moved toward her. Her exposed ankles looked smooth and her skirt had crept up her legs. I passed to steal a look at her face but my gaze dropped downwards, beyond her opened knees. A glint of her was captured like a frame in a movie reel—no undergarments, just a patch of hair surrounded by bare skin.

I turned around and dropped my books to sit, searching my pockets for a cigarette, but she didn't take notice. I cleared my throat and pointed my cigarette at her. "Could I kindly get a light off your cigarette?"

She turned her head, glanced, and then went back to her

book as if I were a passing irritation. Her square face was handsome, the long straight hair tucked behind her right ear. She was thin but her frame was large. Large eyes, too.

"Hun," I said, "I'm an architect; I've been cooped up in Sibley since classes began; I've been on my drawing board with a ruler, pencil, and eraser so long my eyeballs sting. I escape only to sleep, eat and crap, and not necessarily in that order. I haven't been with a woman since I left Baltimore, and I'm profoundly aroused just sitting next you. Now, can I have a light?"

"What'd you say?" she growled.

"Jesus H," I said.

She smiled and extended her cigarette.

"Ah, that's much better," I said. I took my time and watched the smoke roll out of my mouth. I was trying to frame my next line when she closed her book, *The Ghost-Dance Religion*. "My name is Cloud."

She studied me as if I were a lab specimen. "That was a pretty good line," she finally said. "Are you an Indian?"

"Pawnee."

She examined me some more. "You from a reservation out west?"

"Baltimore," I told her.

"Baltimore? A Pawnee from Baltimore?" She squinted. "Do you have a first name, or do you stop with your Indian appellation?"

"Well, what's your name?" I said.

"Carol Pemberton. Greenwich, Connecticut. Second year

Anthro. And I like tuna fish on toasted rye. Okay?"

I figured it was better to stay on the offense with this chick. The smug ones tend to trample you if let 'em. "Let me guess. WASP. Old money. Atheist, maybe Unitarian. Won't date proletariats. How am I doing?"

She wasn't angry. "Not bad, got three out of four. And I like a good stereotype."

She was beginning to dig me, no question in my mind. And I figured the only wrong guess was the one about not dating the working class. I can really be good at times, I thought. I had her attention and now I had to bring her in. I decided to make a connection with anthropology, link me into the discussion, and bring in sex. After that, it should be a cakewalk.

"Are you really a Pawnee, from Baltimore?"

"Carol, I'm a little tight right now and I could use something to eat, and since you're rich, you can treat me to some coffee and fries at the Dragon. And yes, I'm a Pawnee."

She got up. "You don't know I'm rich but come on. You can tell me all about how a Pawnee ended up in Baltimore."

The Green Dragon was a little coffee shop in Sibley's basement. Lunch was over and students were either in class or in their studio. Carol ordered her tuna fish and a Tab, and I grabbed an order of onion rings and Coke. She paid.

I'd never thought of my family as particularly interesting or even different, but Carol was expecting some drama or at the very least a story that would live up to "a Pawnee from Baltimore." Most of my family knowledge came in little vignettes I had picked up as a kid from my grandmother.

The Pawnee line came from my grandfather, who was a recruit of the Carlisle School in Pennsylvania. The school was a government experiment to educate Indians. It wasn't successful, and most of the recruits returned to the reservations in Oklahoma with useless skills, like reading and math. My grandfather didn't return to Oklahoma but stayed to marry my Quaker grandmother, who was working as a nurse in the school's dispensary and was already with child. About that time war broke out in Europe, and my grandfather joined the American Expeditionary Forces to fight in France. He caught a bullet in the chest near Verdun.

My grandmother raised my father, who ended up an EBDB—East Baltimore Delinquent Boys. I don't think he got into serious trouble but he was difficult. He dropped out of school and enlisted in the Navy at seventeen, proved himself in the Pacific, and after the Japanese surrendered stayed in the service, assigned to different ports. During a short furlough in Charleston, he met and married my mother, a Southern belle.

I couldn't tell if Carol was impressed or entertained by my genealogy, but she chewed slowly on her tuna fish. She made eye contact, locked, looked down, and locked again. She barely moved her head, only to lift her coffee to her mouth. "What is your name? Your first name?" she finally said.

"Joseph, just like my father and grandfather. But everyone calls me Joe."

"Hollywood loves the Cheyenne and the Sioux, but the

Pawnees have always been my favorite Plains tribe. They were the most advanced, the most sophisticated, and they had agriculture. The first farmers."

She was brandishing her knowledge but also telling me she was interested. "You know Carol, in the Pawnee tradition, when boys reached puberty, they were paired with an older woman. They would live together and the woman would teach the boy all he needed to know. The boy in turn would provide all her needs. I suppose that's the sophistication you were talking about." I didn't know if this was true. I didn't think I had heard this from my grandmother, I may have read it. Regardless, it was worth a shot.

"The practice isn't uncommon, but I don't know how widespread that was in their culture," Carol said matter-of-factly. "It's an advanced form of sexual development, still practiced today in some cultures."

"The Pawnees were also openly polygamous," I said.

"Are you a polygamy advocate?"

"Not at all. I'm strictly a one-at-a-time man myself."

"Well, I could be convinced of polyandry," she said, then laughed.

"What's that?"

"The practice of a female having more than one mate at a time. Polygamy is when the spouse of either sex has more than one mate at a time; polygyny is the practice of a male having more than one female mate at one time."

"Yeah?"

"It wouldn't work," she said. "I mean polyandry. One guy would always be trying to knock off the other guy and might eventually succeed. That's why you don't find cultures with that practice, while polygyny is quite prevalent. I suppose we females are more tolerant."

"Are you sure there haven't been any cultures that have practiced polyandry?"

"Well, there have been tolerant cultures, but I don't know of any truly polyandrous ones."

"Listen, are you busy tonight?"

"I've got a date."

"Well, that's okay," I said. "You're a polyandry proponent. I won't mind if he doesn't."

She laughed. "No, no. I mean I've got a resident advisor's meeting at the dorms this evening."

I wasn't going to give up after that. "All right. How about tomorrow?"

"Now, what have you got in mind?"

"You can come to my dorm room and we can grab some pizza—I'll treat, and you can sneak in a good California Chablis. I'll fill you in on Pawnees. How's that?"

"I don't think I've ever been to the men's dorm," she said, with some hesitation "I've been to fraternities and apartments but never to the dorms."

She was thinking only freshmen live in the dorms, and who wanted to go out with a freshman? I could have told her I had worked as a draftsman for two years after high school and was older than she, but since I already snagged her, I'd save it for later.

I walked her to her dorm, a Tudor Gothic building overlooking Fall Creek Gorge. The rooms featured all sorts of turn-of-the-century remnants, including secret stairwells, dumbwaiter shafts, and room fireplaces. The RA job was generally reserved for upperclassmen. How did a sophomore connive her way to a resident advisor job? When we entered the main lounge, Carol promised me a bottle of wine and told me to pick her up tomorrow at 7:30. She then turned toward the stairs.

I studied her, tall and graceful, with short steps. "Carol, how about a kiss," I blurted. "After all we've been through polyandry and polygyny."

She turned and came to me as if to retrieve a forgotten book. Her long arms curled around my neck, and she smothered me with a deep kiss. I tasted her thick tongue, my hands timorously on her hips.

"Damn," I said disengaging.

"See you tonight, big boy."

WHEN I RETURNED to the dorms, Harold was at his desk, typing on his Remington and chomping on potato chips. An unopened Orange Nehi sat in front of him.

"If you aren't going to drink the soda, I'll take it," I said. "By the way, can you get yourself lost tomorrow night?"

"You can have half," he said, handing me the can and a glass. "Why? You got a date?"

"We're going to have a candlelit pizza dinner with some cheap California wine, and I'll need the room probably till eleven."

Harold was also in the architecture program. Since classes had begun, he had been kicked out of the room only twice—that's how busy they've kept us.

I expected him to agree without any thought, but Harold paused a minute then began to negotiate. "You know it's very unlikely I'll ever have anyone up in this room on a Friday or Saturday night, and if I'm gonna get kicked out of my room regularly...That doesn't seem quite fair."

"Harold, if you want to start going out with women, you've got to make an effort. They're not just going to line up at your door, you understand what I'm saying, buddy?"

"That's just it," he whined, "I don't know how to make an effort. I've never even been out with a girl in my life. I think about them and look at them all the time. I, I...I have no idea. Period."

I just looked at him. He was probably telling the truth, maybe a little nerdy, but then the whole damn campus was full of nerds. I'm sure he was pent up like everyone else. Harold had several back issues of *Playboy* in his desk, all tousled and stained with covers unhinging from the staples.

"God, if only you could give me some pointers," he said. "I could really pick things up from you. Golly, Joe, you're the only freshman on campus who's got women falling all over. Any chance I can join the party?"

"What? No damn way. There's no way you are going to mess up my evening tomorrow, Harold. You hear me, buddy?"

39

"What if I can figure out a way of not interfering with you two?"

"What the hell do you mean?"

"Look, I've got an idea," he began, voice elevated. "I can stay hidden in the closet. I'll have the closet curtains drawn and I won't make a sound."

I thought about it for a moment.

Harold continued. "I'll learn from you—how to talk to them, what to say, and how to time my moves."

I laughed out loud. "What are you? A pervert?"

"Wait Joe, it's a great idea and it'll work. I'll be able to hear everything, and I'll learn in one evening what could take me years. Look, I'll admit it—I'm a virgin. You're the biggest stud in the dorms. Please?"

"You can't just sit on the floor for three hours. What if you have to piss or even sneeze or cough?"

"No, no," he said. "I'll have a handkerchief or something to stuff in my mouth. I won't make a sound. Really."

I laughed then lit a cigarette. I thought a minute; I almost felt sorry for him and he had been an okay roommate. I had a good idea Carol would come through tomorrow, and I'd more than likely forget about Harold in the closet. And what he said about me was true—I did have a reputation as an ass-man in the dorms.

"Okay," I heard myself saying. "But there are conditions, Harold."

"Anything."

"First, this is between you and me, no one else knows. Second, if you make a sound, and I mean any sound, I'll bust your damn kneecaps. And three, you buy the pizza for us. Large pepperoni with mushrooms and black olives. You can get it from the hot truck outside."

"Deal," Harold snapped.

"And Harold, go to Collegetown and get a couple of fat candles. Atmosphere's important."

I had misgivings, but I shook them off. Besides, Harold might be right, he might learn something. On top of that, I was getting a pizza dinner out of it. I did wonder how Harold would handle the discomfort, keeping still in a two-by-four stuffy closet for several hours.

We worked out the logistics. By 7:45 sharp, Harold would have the pizza in the room and have the two candles lit, and he would also have his stereo on. I had reminded him again the importance of our schedule, and by the agreed time, he would be in the closet with the curtains drawn. And he would remain dead still.

CAROL WAS LATE. She had the girl at the front desk of her dorm to have me wait for her. I grabbed a seat on a Victorian sofa and picked up a copy of the *Daily Sun* from the coffee table. The lobby was busy. Every man had to come to the desk and announce himself, and then the desk girl would telephone the date, and he'd have to wait. I watched them. Some paced and others straightened their ties or smoothed their slacks.

I played a little game. I scrutinized the callers and guessed who was on a first date, a blind date, or a repeat date. It wasn't difficult. Out of the six samples, I correctly guessed all of them. Two were blind dates—they were dressed in tweed jackets or blazers, hair slicked down, and they paced like caged animals. When the coed came downstairs, it was always a "Hi Marilyn? I'm Steve," or a "Hello, are you Doris?" The expression on the girl was even better, an animated "Hi, John?" or a surprised "Oh." On first dates, both of them had nervous smiles or giggled with an "Are we ready?"

Carol finally came into the lobby after eight. "I'm really sorry, Joe. Stopped to pick up a bottle." She lifted a brown paper bag. She looked prettier than I remembered, and taller— about my height.

By the time we walked into my room, the pizza was lukewarm, but Harold had two candles lit. And the room was clean and picked up. The Temptation's latest LP was on the stereo, and Smokey Robinson was singing. I glanced at the closet, sensing Harold's increased heartbeat. Poor Harold, he'd already been lying squeezed in the closet for about three quarters of an hour.

The room had two chairs, two beds, and two desks. Carol plopped down on my bed and said, "This is nicer than I thought. Where's your roommate?"

"We must have just missed him. I told him to turn on the stereo and light the candles before he left. I think he went out with the guys on the floor, and they'll probably be out till midnight."

I flipped the pizza box cover—a large pizza with pepperoni, mushroom and black olives. The vegetables looked dried, but the pepperoni still had tiny yellow grease bubbles caught in the indentations. Harold had placed a couple of paper plates and napkins on his desk—nice touch, but there were no wine glasses, not even drinking glasses. I took the California Chablis out of the brown bag, twisted the metal cap and sniffed the bottle. "Smells good, but I'm afraid we don't have any drinking glasses."

"That's all right," she said. "We can swig it right out of the bottle. It's on the sweet side, perfect for pizza."

God, I like this woman, I thought. I went to lock the door. Women's visiting hours were for Saturday nights only, but few freshmen were able to take advantage of it. Instead, weekend nights were usually spent at Collegetown bars or just hanging out with each other in the dorms.

Carol was in a good mood as Smokey purred away. The candles flickered and cast their shadows onto the walls like a Chinese paper cut-out play. The heat came on, the iron radiators knocking every few minutes. I caught Carol studying me as I handed her a slice on a plate. She leaned against the headboard with her legs stretched out, drinking wine and chewing her pizza. I revisited images of her undergarments, or lack thereof, but then I would hear, or imagine, sounds from the closet. Thoughts of Harold would surface—suffocating in the closet, probably thirsty, and needing to move his cramped limbs. Or worse, to scratch his back or take a piss. I shook off those thoughts, I had more important things to think about, and do.

Carol made small talk, then sketched her life in Greenwich. She had moved from Manhattan about the time she had precociously reached puberty. Her cramps were unbearable and the sickness in the mornings was so fierce she'd throw up and often miss school. She went to the library for medical books on menstruation and anatomy, also masturbation. Before long she began to experiment and she was hooked. The photographs she had seen in the books only spurred her, and from there she began to wet her fingers. She had read a translated Japanese novel describing climax as "clouds and rain." She told me the description was close.

Carol was getting loaded. She reclined flat on her back, legs straight, pillow under her head; I was on the floor next to her. It was time, I thought, and stood up. She looked at me and stopped talking. I sat down on the bed next to her, bent forward, and pressed my lips to hers. At first she held me lightly as if I was fragile, but soon she rolled over on me. I felt the brunt of her weight.

She sunk her tongue into my mouth and began to grind her hips with her hands under my bottom. I tried to chase her movements as if I were being led in a tango. We panted. She lifted her hips to unbuckle my belt, and I followed to unbutton her blouse and unclip her brassiere. She then knelt between my legs and slid my pants down.

The candles fluttered and danced. I was set to take over the lead and tried to get up, but Carol wouldn't have it. She had my shoulders pinned by her long limbs, her tongue brushing my lips and then moving downwards. When she took me into her mouth, I shrieked and then moaned help-lessly, louder against her silence. Again I signaled her to change positions, but again she kept control and overwhelm-ed me like an assailant.

Carol straddled me. I arched my back and she took my flesh to hers. She leaned forward to kiss me once more, both arms wrapped around my neck. Still on my back, I began to thrust back and forth with my feet flat on the bed. Carol pushed back, her hips shoved into me like a provoked wrestler. I yielded. This isn't like me, I thought, and I pictured Harold's ear against the cotton curtains imagining his hero in a submissive position.

With her eyes closed and head tilted, she began a slow rhythmic motion, raising and lowering herself using her knees to pivot. I looked at her. She was in a trance, absorbed and self-focused. She then moved her fingers to her mouth, moistening them and lowering them to herself. She accelerated her rhythm to a higher frequency—her body and her breathing—as if she were conducting an orchestra to a pitched climax. My eyes fixed on her neck, the muscles strained and striated. Her dominance gave me pause. I lost my strength, to a withered state. At that moment I heard faint noise from the closet.

Carol didn't stop. Her frustration showed as she tried to revive me as if I was having a cardiac arrest. Her spurtive movements only killed any chances. I was embarrassed, not only because of my inadequacy, but because Harold was probably biting his tongue to keep from laughing—the bastard was probably having the time of his life. Then I reasoned it was all his fault—that damn Harold—him and his crazy idea. Strangling him crossed my mind.

As I tried a feeble apology, Carol got up and grabbed the wine, taking a long swig.

"Let's go," she said. "Might as well call it a night."

Looking up from bed, she loomed larger, her shoulders broader, her face more resolute—I, depleted. I glanced at the closet again.

The campus street lamps glimmered yellow. The night was brisk, the late October air hinting of what lay ahead, the familiar crickets silent. Carol wasn't mad at me but she didn't say much walking back to her dorm. I thought about discussing the evening's events, but to what end? We made small talk about the coming cold weather and our class deadlines. After saying good night she gave me a light peck on my cheek, smiling feebly.

When I returned to my dorm, I found Harold reading in bed, a half-eaten pizza on his night table. I tossed my jacket down and blew up. "Shit, what a fucked up evening!"

"Why? What happened?"

"What the hell do you mean by what happened? You heard the whole damn thing, didn't you?"

"Joe, I wasn't here," he said, looking innocent as hell. "I stayed in that cramped closet forever, and you didn't show up, so I went drinking with the guys at the Chapter House."

"Harold, are you telling me you weren't in the closet?"

"No," he said. "When I got back from the bar, the door was

still locked, so I stayed in Murphy's room until you and Carol left. Look, when I left the dorm, I left the candles and the stereo on just in case. I hope all of that was all right."

There was a pause.

"Why, won't she see you again?"

I plopped down on my bed. What the hell was I supposed to say to him—that I was relieved he hadn't been in the closet?

"The chick's messed up, Harold," I said. "Pass over the rest of your pizza."

PHOTO SHOT

EVEN THOUGH THAT November morning in '67 was freezing cold, the lecture obscenely early, and the class a dreaded requirement, Professor Weller got my attention when he walked to the podium, laid down his lecture notes, cleared his throat and asked, "Does anyone know why sewer tops are round?"

The steam heat baked the amphitheater like an oven,

leaving some two hundred students in Baily Hall in a listless state. He brings up sewer tops, I thought, and this is a psychology class? Even the sycophants in the front were dumbfounded.

"Well, it's early in the morning," the professor continued, "and I thought I'd start by jostling your left hemisphere. And it looks like no one..." He spotted a hand near the front and stopped. "Someone's not asleep." He pointed his finger. "Yes?"

"The circle is the only geometric shape that keeps the top from falling through the hole," the student answered.

"Good," Weller said. "Now we can move on to today's lecture."

That someone looked like Kay Winchcombe. I had first spotted her on campus walking across the lawn between classes. She'd stood out, tall like a Madison Avenue model, proud with defined jaws and angular features. Her face was ceramic white with shades of pink around her cheeks and nose. But it was her eyes that you'd first notice—cold blue, bordered by dark lashes and angled brows. Her long hair was jet-black, and she carried herself like a Marine out of boot camp, chest forward and stomach in. What a model she'd be for a photo shoot, I had thought.

I hadn't had an eight o'clock since my freshman year, but *Psychology of Deviance* was not your run-of-the-mill course. Students referred to it as *Nuts and Sluts*, Professor Harvey Weller's flagship course. He was a morning person, it was said, and all his classes were early, and he saved his little pearls for the first part of his lectures.

I am not a morning person. I'd get the midnight munchies, step out for a pizza, smoke a butt or two, and read myself to sleep. I have trouble with Ben Franklin's "early to bed and early to rise" advice.

That morning I sat in the back of the lecture hall up in the tiered seats, and Weller's little drama kept me awake for a while, but his prepared lecture began to sound like a lullaby. My eyelids grew heavy, my pencil heavier.

Weller spotted my head and torso seesawing like an oil rig and stopped mid-sentence, and then he sprinted up the steps. When he reached me, he slapped a dime on my desk. I looked up groggily.

"Son, go and get a cup of coffee," the professor commanded in a stage-whisper. He turned and descended to the podium. The lecture hall buzzed.

I picked up the dime and walked down the steps, eyes on the door. When I reached the podium level, I looked up to see Weller's grin. Humiliation set in.

I left class and ambled down the hall toward the vending machines. The dime jangled down the dispenser, and the coffee dripped, steam escaping from the cup. I felt like an actor missing a line, all too obvious to the audience. I couldn't just disappear off the stage, I could only continue, gracefully.

I returned to the lecture hall, crossed the floor, set the cup on the podium, and sauntered up the stairs to my desk. Weller stopped his lecture and watched as the class clapped in unison.

My intention was not to embarrass the professor, and I didn't think I had. When the lecture finished, I slowly stood, safe in the amplified commotion and chatter, and moved down the steps. I recognized the coed who had shamed us earlier. It was Kay.

"That was an interesting display," I heard the professor say as I walked past the podium. "Your name?"

"Jared, sir," I said, turning to him. "Jared Bowman."

"Well, Mr. Bowman, I must say I was impressed with your theatrics, especially since you were half asleep. Are you a photographer?"

I could have said the same of his little melodrama. After all, how many professors propel themselves up a 30 degree incline to give a dime to a student at eight in the morning? Evidently he had noticed my Nikon strapped to my shoulder, and I wondered if this was a setup before the hammer came down.

"Yes sir, it's a hobby."

"I have a research project that could use a photographer. Interested?"

"Yes sir," I said, surprised.

"Come to my office at Morrill Hall tomorrow noon, and I'll fill you in."

I was an art history major, not psychology. But I supposed it didn't matter as long as the job paid. There were plenty of photographers on campus, but Weller had asked me. I brought him that coffee through some built-in groggy auto response, and as it turned out, it was like an snapshot that turned out to be a showpiece.

Too many art history majors are disappointed artists devoid of talent. Growing up, I had taken drawing, painting, and even sculpture lessons, but my talent just wasn't there. When I was twelve, my grandfather gave me a Brownie camera. I liked the little pictures I picked up at the drugstore—the perforated squares, black and whites with the dates stamped on them. Later, I'd taken photography courses, but I was bored by the technology of it: F-stops, focal lengths, compensations, shutter speeds. But I had continued to shoot, everything and everyone.

Freshman year I'd taken a photography course, and in a darkened room with diffused red lamps, my papers floated in trays filled with sour chemicals. I'd gently push and pull the tray until the details magically appeared. The first time I saw an image slowly materialize on paper, it seemed like sorcery.

Cropping out, zooming in, dodging, and burning gave me control of my creation. I grew accustomed to, and even depended on, the solitude of the dark room—which was why I couldn't leave my apartment without my camera.

My roommate Railey told me I held my camera lens as if it were a phallus. Psych majors. When I told him about Weller's job offer, he turned to me in disbelief. "No. You're kidding. He usually offers jobs to coeds, and only to good looking ones."

Railey was a nerd from New Jersey. When he talked, his nose twitched like a rabbit. I told Railey about Weller's sewer question and Kay Winchcombe.

"Forget Kay, Jared. She's untouchable," he said. "I know

you're a horny bastard, but every guy in the Psych department has hit on her—and nothing. No one can get to first
base with her, and no one's seen her with anybody."

Railey added she was a loner. She didn't live in the dorms
or in a Collegetown shack like everyone else but had her own
place in a high-rise farther up Dryden Road. She worked as a
lab assistant in the Psych department, though Railey found
that a little curious. From what he'd heard, she was wealthy
and didn't need the money.

PROFESSOR WELLER HAD received his doctorate in psychology from Berkeley by age twenty-three, one of the youngest
to do so. His courses were popular, and he was known for his
flamboyance. Students talked about him as if he were a cele-
brity, and national television liked his panache and interviewed him periodically.

On the first day of my *Deviance* class, there was no lecture.
Instead we watched a movie about a Skinnerian experiment.
Two raised platforms were built on each end of a box, and
the floor was rigged with electric currents. A mouse was
taught to reach the other platform for food and water, even
as the voltage increased during each run. When the shock
became too intense, the mouse refused to cross the floor and
starved to death.

Another mouse was also taught to reach the other
platform, but it had surgically implanted electrodes in its
brain and received ecstasy like an orgasm. Even with
increased jolts and pain, the mouse continued to cross the

floor for its dose of blissful delirium. Eventually, the mouse was shocked to death running to its stimulus.

So, sex is more important than food? Was that the inference? The images of the little mouse continued to emerge in my consciousness, usually triggered by the sight of a pretty coed and sometimes by food.

When I arrived at Weller's office, he was in conference with several coeds, and he gestured for me to wait outside. Decked out in a pin-striped shirt and bow tie, he was in top form. He'd also taken off his wire-rims. I guessed that the coeds were his research team, and he'd interview me alone.

He finally stepped out of his meeting and motioned me to follow him into his office. "Let me tell you where we are, Jared," he said as I sat down. "We need to measure pupil dilation for our project."

"Pupil dilation?"

"See, a few years ago in '65, a Chicago study showed eyes dilate under emotionally charged stimuli. For example, a man might look at a beautiful woman and his pupil size would enlarge. We'll first replicate that study, and then we'll proceed to a hypothesis, and when the time comes, I'll give you details. In the meantime, you can begin to catch up on the literature." He handed me some journal articles, still smelling from mimeograph.

"Interesting," I said.

"We have a problem, though. We have expensive camera equipment, but we're having trouble capturing dilation. We've tried telephoto and close-ups, but measuring them is tricky. You have any thoughts, Jared?"

I had tinkered with close-up photography: flowers, documents, and even insects. Weller was giving me a problem his photographers couldn't solve. The solution wasn't in the equipment.

"Sir, if you have trouble measuring the dilation, it's because you're having trouble distinguishing the black of the pupil and the iris. I would suggest using blue-eyed subjects and using color film rather than black and white. Of course, you'll have to make sure you don't introduce bias."

"You know, people who have an uncommon response to stimuli are uncommon," he said, referencing the coffee incident, I supposed. "My instinct about you was correct. Welcome aboard."

There were reasons why getting the job with Weller made my day. I had at times fantasized about earning a living with photography—a paid artist. Also, I really did need the money, my partial scholarship and loan never enough. And I knew Kay Winchcombe also worked for Weller. If the professor thought I was uncommon, I figured I had a shot with her.

I read everything I could about the Chicago study and experimented with camera lenses, continuous shutters and lighting. Weller had already mapped out the experiment: pictures, sequence and time-duration. The control pictures were buildings, and stimuli were pinups of movie stars. He even had nudes.

Weller collected blue-eyed volunteers: students, teaching

assistants, and even instructors. Recording the changes in pupils was like working a lie detector, revealing hidden thoughts and feelings. And my suggestion to use color film worked better than expected.

Student volunteers were given a questionnaire about their background, but they were not provided the purpose of the experiment. When coeds looked at a picture of a handsome man in a swimsuit, their pupils enlarged; the men were even more predictable.

Then Kay Winchcombe came in. There were no introductions as the assistants proceeded to explain the procedure and gave her the standard instructions. I avoided any obvious stare, and there was no eye contact. Kay just nodded at the directions and said nothing—no facial expressions at all, as if she was reading a grocery receipt. I couldn't tell for certain, but as the camera clicked away I didn't think her pupils changed. Pictures of attractive men of all sorts but no reaction. I found her detachment difficult to tell whether it was a conscious effort, but the developed photos confirmed what I had observed.

There were several cases like Kay's—no responses at all. The subjects and their results were identified by case numbers, and there was anonymity. Even Weller did not know how individual subjects tested, though I did.

The professor was drawn by the unresponsive cases. "Ask the students to come back and show them a different set of stimuli, and vary the range, of course."

The three cases were retested with a wider set of stimuli:

male and female, young and old, black and white, and nudes. Kay's pupils didn't change at all.

"Possible cases of asexuality?" an assistant asked during a staff meeting. "We've tried pretty much everything."

Our heads turned toward Weller.

"Possibly," he said. "We don't really know much about asexuality—broadly speaking, lack of sexual attraction or interest in sex. Psychologically induced, more than likely. Kinsey estimated about one and a half percent of the male population to be asexual; he didn't make any female findings and he didn't go further with his research."

I began to think of Kay more—during lectures, while walking, and at night. I'd look for her in-between classes and in dining halls. I admit I had been attracted to her, but her secret gave me an unexplained intimacy—also, when I'd see her on campus, a sense of privileged vantage.

IN ONE OF my photography courses, I made a discovery. We were assigned to take head shots in natural lighting. In the back of my English class, I had spotted a coed by the window. In late afternoon light, my long lens caught her glowing cheeks—her eyes, taut and overwrought. I made a couple of glossies in the darkroom and when the eight-by-tens rolled out of the dryer, other photographers stole glances. I hadn't known the coed before, but when I showed her the pictures, she was moved. The photos gave me the perfect introduction.

After that, if I sighted a particular coed and an opportunity presented itself, I'd shoot. If not, I'd wait and find out where she stopped for coffee, ate her meals, or walked to classes. I'd purchased a lens adapter to photograph at 90 degrees from where my lens pointed—a spy lens. When I'd catch her in the right light, I'd shoot. I'd develop the pictures, present them to her, and watch her eyes widen, most of the time in pleasure and gratitude.

When I revealed my secret to Railey, he paused. "I get it. So that's why you've been going out so much—Margo, Dana, Gretchen. Very good."

He proceeded to pontificate. "When you present your subject with pictures, flattering and glamorous, she falls in love with herself. Then she transposes that love to you—the creator. It's called transference."

I thought Railey's explanation was psycho-wacko gibberish, whatever the label. It didn't always work, but it beat going to bars in Collegetown.

I KNEW KAY often stopped for coffee in the student union building in the afternoons. It was a perfect ambush spot—bright afternoon lights through tall windows. The room was uncongested but crowded enough to camouflage me. I loaded my camera with Tri-X film and waited. During the second week, I found her alone, lost in reading with a coffee in her hand, low sunlight striking her from the side. I aimed my telephoto lens and fired.

She was naturally photogenic with her defined features stark and contrasty. The camera captured her ephemeral moods: blank stares, intense frowns, and even boredom. The grey smoke from her cigarette lent a dreamlike quality.

The following week, I saw her again at the same table and introduced myself. I told her I worked in the psychology department and that I had met her as the photographer of the project. She remembered me.

"An interesting project Weller's working on," she said. "What's the hypothesis?"

"I really can't divulge that right now," I said. "But I saw you here last week and I took some shots of you."

"Yeah, I know. I spotted you."

When I showed her the pictures, she examined them like a critic—carefully, taking her time. "These are good, quite good," she finally said. "You have a good eye."

"Thanks, you can keep them. I have to tell you that you make a good model. I was wondering if you would consider posing. It'd only take an hour of your time, and I'd of course give you copies of the pictures."

She declined, thanking me for the pictures, and left.

The next Monday morning, I caught her eye in Weller's class and sat behind her. I studied the back of her head, her long neck, and lustrous skin. I think she sensed my stare, periodically looking askance as if to see me from the corner of her eye.

When class broke, I tailgated her as she moved toward the door. Before I spoke, she turn to me. "Jared, I've thought over your offer," she said. "If you'd still like to take some shots of me, I'd be interested."

"Sure, I'd like a session."

"I'd have to insist on a couple of conditions," she said. "You must not show the photos to anyone but me. Never. And, I determine the poses, not you."

I didn't particularly like the conditions, but I was sure she was adamant. Besides I was going to have time with her, alone. We agreed to meet Wednesday at three at the student union, and we'd go to my apartment. Before we parted, she reaffirmed her conditions. "And remember, the pictures are for my eyes only," she growled. "And yours." Her jaw lines tightened, threatening.

For the next two days, anticipation filled my head. I restrained myself and didn't tell Railey of our engagement, knowing he'd be in class that afternoon. My Eddy Street apartment faced west and the light would add to the shoot. I imagined her poses, her proximity, and her intimacy.

On Wednesday a warm front passed through, the clouds low and the air thick with fine mist. Our faces and hair were wet by the time we reached my apartment. I had tidied the living room in the morning, and the dull afternoon light broke through the windows casting a lambent gloss on the walls. Kay surveyed the room, taking off her jacket to sit on the sofa.

I explained the importance of a photographer-subject rapport and suggested we continue our small talk, and I placed a kettle on the stove for tea. She seemed to understand and immediately began to ask me about my interests, my photography, and my studies. She wanted to pre-empt any queries of her.

She picked up the canvas bag she had brought and excused herself to the bathroom. When she returned she had changed her blouse—creamy and delicate with frills around her neck and front. She had also rearranged her hair.

"This belonged to my mother," she said as she moved to the window. She looked out to the street, her hands down and clasped. Her head tilted slightly down. "Do you think you could imitate those old-time photos?"

She had planned her poses, I thought. Her gazes were blank and unfocused. The room was silent but for the metallic clicking of my shutter. Kay gradually changed positions, shifting her weight and turning her head slowly. I finished off the roll and opened my camera to reload.

"I'd like to try something different," she said looking at me. "I'd like you to shoot some nudes."

I concealed my surprise. "If you'd like. I have to tell you I've never done any."

"It's okay," she reassured me. "Do you have a bed in this apartment?"

My bed was unmade, a pile of rumpled white sheets with the blanket on the floor. She turned her back to me as she slipped off her blouse, then her brassiere and her panties. She sat on the bed and moved her weight to her elbow and hip, lying on her side, and then she used her other arm to pull the bed sheet to cover her legs and only half of her rear. I wanted to adjust the camera shutter speed, but my fingers wouldn't cooperate. I tried desperately not to swallow, as I didn't want to reveal my arousal.

She looked at me to signal she was ready. I had seen the pose before in artsy photographs and girly magazines. Her white body seemed to meld with the sheets, accentuating her black hair and eyebrows. She looked lovingly at the camera.

After a handful of clicks, she changed positions and sat with her legs pressed to her breasts, her hands wrapped around her ankles. She moved only her head as I fired away. After my last frame, I sat next to her and placed my clammy hand on her back.

"Please, don't," she said and abruptly stood up to dress. "I really don't have any interest in that."

"I've been thinking about you for quite a while now."

"It's not part of our agreement," she said flatly and finished dressing.

She reminded me again that no one else was to see the photos and even mentioned the need for privacy in the darkroom. Through my window I watched her walk briskly up the street, and from afar she seemed spirited and vigorous. Her lab results were so incongruous, I thought, but her reaction to my touch had confirmed her pupils.

Early Saturday morning I processed the film in the darkroom with only one other student using the facility. The black and whites of Kay were magnificent, some of my best portraits. One close-up of her in her mother's blouse caught her with a scant smile looking tenderly at the camera, and another showed her eyes, somehow seeming intelligent and breathing with life. The nudes were suggestive and in good taste, her body lines against the sheets like a charcoal drawing. There's a debate of what constitutes a great photograph—the subject or the craftsmanship, and in this case it was clearly the subject.

When I told her in class that the pictures were finished, she seemed eager to see them and asked if she could come to the apartment that afternoon. Kay was unduly punctual, and without preliminaries, I handed her the manila envelope with the photographs.

Before she opened it, she looked at me. "Jared, I'd appreciate very much if you'd give me the negatives also. And of course I'll pay for the expenses."

I was ready for this. "Sure, they're yours. And don't worry about the expenses, it wasn't much."

Unlike her previous visit, the room was filled with sunlight, its glare bouncing off the walls and ceiling. She sat next to me on the sofa and smiled before opening the envelope.

Her movements were deliberate and measured. She studied each picture, taking her time, her head changing positions as if she were searching for something. She wore a fixed, faint smile, and it was when she looked at the nudes that I noticed her pupils, fully dilated against her blue iris. I feigned my glances, moving my head to look around the room only to catch her pupil on my way to the photos. There was no doubt, her pupils had widened. She was aroused. Now, to take advantage of Railly's transference. I unhurriedly turned my head behind her and moved my mouth toward her neck.

She sprang up. "What is it with you?" she shouted angrily.

"I'd told you clearly that I wasn't interested."

"Yeah, I already know," I said quietly.

"And what do you mean by that?" she said, her expression changing.

My response was stupid and impetuous, and I would have given anything to take it back. But the milk was spilled. "Weller's project linked pupil dilation with arousal. And your reaction..."

She stared at me for what seemed to a full minute, though I'm sure it wasn't. She grabbed her things and left, slamming the door behind her. I sat on the sofa, fixed.

I didn't see much of her for the rest of the semester. She often cut Weller's class or sat in the back. And I never saw her again at the student union. A month into the second semester, Railey told me the Psych department got word she would not be returning to school. He had heard rumors she had been in a car accident or she had jumped out of a moving car—an apparent suicide attempt. No one knew for certain the extent of her injuries.

I went to my room and stared at my bed. Then I retrieved the hidden folder with Kay's photos, and examined them as if for the first time. I began to rip her prints, first in half, then into hundreds of pieces—fragments of hair, skin and eyes. The little pieces were like a heap of mosaic tiles in my wastebasket.

COWBOY

IN 1966, WHAT was more curious than a Chinaman with a Southern drawl in upstate New York in the middle of a blizzard? Back then there were only a scant number of Asians on campus, mostly international students in graduate studies.

The snowstorm ravaged the campus but few were concerned. It was exam week. I had claimed a carrel next to a window in the stacks, and I could see the snow riding the screaming gusts. Beside me a steam pipe hissed. Next to the student union building, the library was a quiet place to study, with stacks resembling a mouse maze of bookshelves and tiny cubicles. I knew the library well, having to work at the checkout desk sixteen hours a week. Like others I had a partial scholarship and loan supplemented by a student employment program. Counting nickels and dimes had become routine, though it was a constant reminder of my meager budget.

FAR FROM THE library, Texas was my home. Henry Heung, my father, had fought with the Nationalist Army under Chiang Kai-shek against the CPC—Communist Party of China—in the late 1940s. The Communists defeated Chiang's army and drove them out to sea and eventually to the island of Taipei. From there my father was able to get to the United States, but no one seems to know the details. In those days the immigration policy of the United States only allowed 105 Chinese to enter the country annually. He had told me there was a clause in the immigration laws that allowed "refugees" to circumvent the quota and that Chiang personally assisted in pushing his paperwork. My guess is my father knew the right people to pay off; back then, many had evaded the quota system through this loophole. At six years of age, I entered the port of San Francisco with my father and mother. I don't remember much, though I do have images of tall buildings and nights as bright as day. My father found work as a waiter in a restaurant, but soon ran into an old army general he had served under during the last years of the Communist push. The general, who managed to enter his new country with a suitcase of greenbacks, had partnered with an American ex-army colonel to own the largest Chinese restaurant in San Antonio. My father accepted the general's invitation to move his family to Texas to work for the Golden Dragon Restaurant.

By high school the only foreign language I spoke was French, having forgotten Shanghainese during my years in Texas. There weren't many of us in San Antonio in the Fifties. Eager for me to be an American, my father encouraged only English. I learned Texan real quick.

At first the tow-headed boys in the neighborhood didn't know exactly what to think of us. Some thought we were Japs and threw raw eggs at our house when no one was looking. Others, who had seen Charlie Chan movies, thought Orientals were all inscrutable Ching Chang Charlies who ate chop suey. Then there were those who thought we were quaint or mysterious. After a while, and after we became familiar, they viewed us more as kind of a local asset, like having sextuplets living on their street.

I couldn't speak much English on the first day of school in Mrs. Coleman's second grade class. Our teacher, tall and bony and about to retire, had blue hair and bright-red lipstick, which I found strange. In Asia women stopped wearing makeup after marriage. Looking back, she probably said in her twangy and vibrating voice, "Class, this is Jimmy Heung. He's from China, but he's not a Communist. I want you all to treat him like a guest. Remember, the Chinese people welcomed Marco Polo with their hospitality, and we must do the same." She probably said it to protect me from lynching.

During recess, the class bully took me aside and gave me a miniature pocketknife. It was a kind gesture from the burly class hood. He didn't say anything, just winked.

The kids crowded a Good Humor truck after school. I stood and watched, not having any idea what an ice cream was. A little redheaded girl, orange Creamsicle smeared on her face, purchased one for me. She said nothing as she handed me the frozen gift, as if she was returning the favor for the noodles presented to Marco Polo. The ice cream was scrumptious, and I felt I was discovering strange foods and customs, just like the Venetian traveler did so many centuries before.

My father had an accent and so did I. His was Shanghainese, mine was Texan. My dorm mates started off calling me "Cowboy," and I didn't fight the new name. I'd learned long ago that in a foreign setting you go with the flow. But there were advantages to being an Oriental in the land of cattle and sagebrush. Some blonde Texans thought my slanty eyes were exotic, and I exploited every advantage, like a gambler on a winning streak.

EARLIER IN THE MORNING, I had told my roommate I would meet him for lunch. I pressed against the library door as the gale pushed me back. The snow had eased but you couldn't guess it was noon; winds wailed under the gruesome clouds, as the hooded and stooped students shuffled along as if they were on ice. The snow melted on my face. I cleared my eyes with my bare hand, then shoved it back into my warm pocket. Rows of elm trees on Central Avenue had formed tall, gothic-like arches. The gusts redirected the wet snow, pasting it onto the branch tops to form a long, cavernous tunnel, like something out of an early Alfred Stieglitz photograph.

When I pulled open the heavy, wood doors of the student union building, a blast of heated air hit me like exhaust from a tanker truck. The building was packed. In the cafeteria I grabbed a cheeseburger and coffee, thought about adding a plate of French fries, but decided to save myself the twenty cents. Escaping the long line, I spotted my roommate, Zweig.

Isadore Jeffrey Zweig didn't like his first name. He had told me it sounded effeminate. He tried to have everyone call him Jeffrey, but that was too confusing because the teachers announced his name as Isadore. So people just called him Zweig, and that was fine with him.

Zweig was a worrier about everything: school, money, women, even his hair falling out prematurely. His semester schedule had been mapped out before it started—study hours, eating hours, sleeping hours, and socializing hours. Everything needed to be under his control and to be neat, like his room. He and I were at the opposite ends of the Myers-Briggs Personality Test. I liked Zweig, he reminded me of my father. About half of marriages fail in America, and I would guess the chance of successful roommate pairings were about the same.

I spotted Zweig reading the morning paper as I wove through the lunchtime crowd. Snow melted on students' jackets, and I took in the distinct whiff of B.O. in the heavy, evaporated air.

"How'd you do, boy?" I asked him, taking a seat across from him.

"Hey, Cowboy," Zweig said, looking up from the *Daily Sun*. "It wasn't bad. I think I did all right."

We'd taken most of our exams together, except for calculus. Zweig had taken the advanced level course, and his exam had been scheduled earlier.

"Damn, there are more asses in this room than a Texas ranch," I said, my eyes taking a panoramic sweep. "Half of them sopping from the storm."

"Cowboy, you're the horniest damn Chinaman I've ever known – well, the only Chinaman. What time's your calc exam?"

"In about two hours. My last."

"So, you rushing or what?"

"Don't rightly know," I said. "I ain't sure I can afford to live in a fraternity. In fact I know I can't afford a fraternity. I'd like to just see what all this here's about. Besides, I don't have the dough to go back to Texas during the break, and I might as well get free food at the houses. Anyone from ZBT approached you yet?"

"You know that's not allowed."

"You gotta shot at 'em," I said.

72

"I doubt it. They only want the smooth Jews. They already know who's getting ass."

There were strict rushing rules. Freshman contact by fraternities was not allowed during the first semester, but all fraternities had been busy behind the scenes with dossiers on potential pledges. There were white houses and Jewish houses. When I had first heard those labels, I'd thought Jews weren't considered white. Probably the only place in America where you can belong to a non-white house, and still be white.

The fraternity culture was in transition at the time. Maybe it was the front page racial issues, or maybe it was Vietnam, but many white houses were looking to their Jewish friends for "diversity," as they called it. And even more aggressive were the Jewish houses, now looking for their first goys.

There were all sorts of social fraternities on campus: the smooth houses, the animal houses, jock houses, and turkey houses. And some of these fraternities lived in mansions. The Xi Gamma's were located next to the Arts quad near the gorge; their three story manor looked like a Tudor Gothic Castle, its red brick adorned with polished local shale and limestone. With twenty-four bedrooms and fifteen bathrooms, their palace was embellished with a grand staircase, paneling, and stained glass windows from Europe. The frat members represented old money from San Francisco to New York. No Chinaman in that house.

"There are only half a dozen Jewish houses, but I figure I'll end up in one of them," Zweig said. "Why don't you convert,

Cowboy, and we could join together."

"Yeah, a Chinese Methodist Texan in a house fulla nebbishes. But I guess I might go take a look-see into some of them, for the heck of it."

When rush began Monday evening, we freshmen waited in our rooms, stereo on, dressed casually. Some had specific fraternities in mind, but most just waited for a knock on their door. The suited frats were usually in pairs, and they would come into a room, introduce themselves, and recite their line: "We'd like to extend you an invitation for our smoker tomorrow at 10 o'clock." It was like waiting by the punch bowl to be asked to dance, and at the end of the evening, some people had dozens of invitations, others had none.

Zweig was disappointed that ZBT hadn't invited him, but he received an invitation from all the other Jewish houses and hoped Zebe would ask him the following day. The big surprise on the floor was me. Maybe it was the year of the Chink. I got more offers than anyone, even one from Psi Mu, the jock house on campus—probably because I was a second string coxswain on the freshman crew team. I had trouble imagining myself, a scrawny 130 pounder, with these 250 pound football linemen at a black tie dance.

Smokers were a screening process. The frat brothers assayed us like USDA inspectors going over pork carcasses—our attire, gabbing manners, class, composure, and of course, our looks. Some freshmen prayed that no new zits would surface before these events. Coffee, cigarettes, and finger sandwiches were served along with repetitious stories, jokes and lots of forced laughter.

I made it to three houses the first day, where I stood out like a three-legged horse at a rodeo. Everyone went out of their way to pretend I was no different than anyone else. It was only when I opened my mouth with the slow Texas drawl that some couldn't help but stare. I had to put on an act—that I really wasn't that different from anyone else. The whole process was draining.

When I returned to my dorm, I was exhausted. The snow had ceased and changed from blinding white to pale blue as the sun sank behind West Hill. My clothes reeked of cigarette smoke, and I wanted to shower and change before dinner.

Zweig and Hotch were in the room, dressed in their smoker attire, obviously just returned. Gil Hutchinson, or Hotch, a tall, broad-shouldered farm boy from Minnesota, roomed across the hall from us. He was also a tight end on the freshman football team.

"Hey, Cowboy," Hotch said. "What d'you think about Psi Mu? That's some castle, isn't it?"

"It was all right," I said, hanging up my coat. "I'm kinda thinkin' all this is a lot of cow dung. Shoot, I can't even afford to live in 'em."

"Well, there aren't many Greek houses that serve chow mein," he said, laughing. "God, I would love to pledge Psi Mu."

Even by Texas standards, Hotch was corny. Zweig laughed.

"I went to white houses today, but I might look into the Jewish houses tomorrow," I said. "Maybe I'll get some laughs.

Or, I'll find out what bagels are. How'd'you do, Zweig?"

"Not bad. I liked the STD house,"

"STD? Oh yeah. Ain't that the house that gave us both an invite? I think I'll see 'em tomorrow. What happens now?"

Zweig started to take his dress shoes off. "If they like you, they'll come back tonight to ask you to return. If they don't, it means they dinged you, and you can kiss them off. If you get invited back more than a couple of times and you accept, they vote on you."

"You'll know toward the end of the week," Hotch added. "In some houses only one ding from a member is all it takes to keep you out, and other houses might only take a couple of yes-votes to get you in."

The smooth frats didn't have to make much effort. They sold themselves—their reputation, their grand residences, and their antique cars in the parking lot. Most fraternities went out of their way like real estate brokers: number of dean's list students, exam file cabinets, gourmet cook, proximity to campus, their annual lawn party. One house of engineers even showed off their bunk beds rigged by wires as if it were a suspension bridge, and an animal house showed its collection of 300 bottles of beer from all over the world. Everyone was a salesman.

"I'm hungry," Zweig said. "You guys want to go get something from Collegetown or the pizza truck?"

By the end of the week, I had received a handful of invitations to pledge. I particularly liked the Lambda Omega house, full of architects and theater majors, located behind the Law School. And one house stood out—Sigma Tau Delta was the Jewish house that made an offer to both Zweig and me. They weren't like the smooth Zebes, but the Jewish sororities referred to them as the "good-looking nebbishes." The STD brothers liked to call themselves STUDS.

On the second to last day of Rush Week, I was alone in the room mulling over next year's logistics: a fraternity or an apartment in Collegetown, and there wasn't another option. Zweig had already decided on STD and had gone over to the house for the evening. Chuck Fuerster, a ruddy-faced senior with black-rimmed glasses, was STD's house treasurer, and he came to see me alone; he was waiting acceptance to Wharton Business School and was sure he'd be running Wall Street within ten years.

"Hey, Cowboy," he said, entering my room. He sat down on Zweig's bed and began his small talk. His eyes never stopped moving, darting and shifting like a chameleon with independent and rotating eyes. "Listen," he finally said, "the brothers want you in the house. We know you're on scholarship, and we'll make it easy for you."

I paid attention. The Lambda O's already had told me I could get a job in the kitchen, but with house dues, rent, food and additional expenses for parties, it would still be a stretch for me. "Okay," I said. "What do y'all got in mind?"

"If you'd work in our kitchen five days a week—setting the dinner tables, waiting, busing, and dishwashing—we'll give you room and board."

I tried to conceal my surprise. It was more than generous.

"All right," Chuck continued. "The dishwashing only every other week, and we'll throw in the dues. The only thing you'd have to pay for would be the cost of your dinner dates."

Jesus, what's the catch, I wondered, and slowly nodded.

"You've got a deal," I said and extended my hand.

Chuck continued with his generosity. "Not only that, your Saturday dinner dates at the house will also be on us this semester."

I found out later Zweig had been feeding STD details about my invitations from other houses, especially from Lamda Omega and their financial sweetener, and he had been pushing them hard to snag me—he probably exaggerated my poon prowess. So I would join the Jewish fraternity, and my financial worries for next year would disappear.

When Chuck Fuerster reported back at STD he had snagged me, Zweig later told me the brothers were happy to reel me in. The Rush Committee had been charged to bring in some new blood to change the house image, and they were sure a Chinese poon hound who spoke Texan might just do that. And also, for the first time, a handful of new pledges at the house would be goys.

BEFORE COLLEGE, I had known only one Jew in Texas. Her name was Rachel Berenson and her father owned a small pharmacy. She had been a quiet girl, brown hair and dark-complected. Some students had whispered about her as if she had the measles or webbed fingers, but she moved quietly within her circle of friends. Her lips were stolid while others uttered the Lord's Prayer before class.

Saturday, just before classes began, I went to a dinner for all the new pledges at the house. The large living room was jammed with upper-class brothers, sophomores living in the house, and us new plebes. I stood by the open bar and saw Zweig having a good time across the room. People were paired or in groups, chattering.

A Jewish house. In Texas there had been many times I had the same feeling—a little out of place and self-conscious. Almost everyone was from the New York area, with a smattering from Chicago or Los Angeles. The group looked different than a Texas gathering. Here, darker hair seemed to be the norm, though there were blonds and even a handful of redheads. And then there was the accent overlaid with Yiddish words. Good thing Zweig had been giving me lessons.

I studied the crowd in the living room like I had studied Texans, growing up in my new country. I had spent most of my life in the Lone Star State, and I had become comfortable there. I missed Southern civility and the laid-back cadence, traits which, in Northerners' eyes, came across as insincere and dim-witted. Southerners were friendlier, more receptive, and less guarded than their Northern counterparts. At that moment I yearned for the land of cactus, oil wells, and excess. I was thinking how strange it was that I, who would not look out of place in Shanghai, would be forlorn for charred steak and country-western twangs.

Everyone acted as if I were just another schmo from Long

Island, and they worked hard to avoid eye contact. I could still feel their stares, though. Next to me a group chuckled in unison. "He actually thought she'd go out with him. Rosenblatt's such a shlemiehl," a lanky guy said, obviously enjoying the attention.

On these occasions there was always a person who'd notice my displaced position and break the ice. It was the same in Texas. I'd be at a church function or a Boy Scout congregation in another city, and people would study me without staring. I knew what they were thinking: What's a Chinaman doing here? Does he speak American? Should I go and talk to him? And most of the people would be timid about introducing themselves. But there was always a person who'd come forward and then everyone would follow. This time it was Steve Gutman, a roly-poly, bespectacled, curly-haired Brooklynite. His lips were naturally parted, as if they were downing spicy food. He'd been looking at me occasionally, looking for an opening to introduce himself.

"Name's Steve Gutman," he said, extending his hand.

"Jimmy Heung."

"You're Cowboy, aren't you?"

"Yeah."

"I wasn't sure whether you weren't Hung Low," Steve said. He laughed at his joke as he draped his arm on my shoulder. "Cowboy, do you know what shlemiehl means?"

Others around us stopped to hear my response. It was as if they'd been waiting to find out who this Cowboy was.

"Uh-uh."

"Listen, Cowboy, there are two things you'll need to live in this house."

Now it seemed the whole living room stopped to listen.

"First, you'll need to be circumcised, and two, you'll need to know Yiddish."

People laughed, but I continued my stone face.

"Now, we might forego the first requirement for you," he exhorted, with his smile turning to a chuckle. "But you'll have to learn Yiddish."

"Aw'raat," I said with a heavy accent and without a smile.

I laid out my Texas drawl on purpose—throw the shock effect early, and everything that follows becomes easier. We were center stage, and Steve finessed my introduction to the house with humor. "And the first words you'll need to know are shlemiehl, schlimazel, and schmuck—very important."

"What's the difference?"

"Okay, listen carefully," Steve said, enjoying the theatrics. "A schlemiel is the guy who spills the soup. And the schlimazel is the guy who gets the soup on his head."

Everyone one laughed. "And," he said raising his index finger and shifting his eyes left and right, "the schmuck's the guy who pees in the toilet after he gets out of a shower."

I laughed.

"Cowboy!" someone yelled from behind. It was Chuck Fuerster, adjusting his black, plastic-rimmed glasses with his left hand, extending his right. "How you doin', boy?" he said, mimicking my accent.

"You know, Chuck, I'd like to thank ya for the offer the

house made. You beat out Lamda Omega's offer and I'm glad I'm here."

"Well, Cowboy, a deal is a deal, and we have a deal. But I'll tell you something. We were ready to offer you even some cash to bring you in. Welcome aboard, partner." He patted me on my shoulder and disappeared into another gathering.

Why the hell did he have to tell me that? The bastard probably *will* run Wall Street in ten years. I had been in this country for twelve years, and the adjustments and shifts I'd made, including learning a new language, seemed like a long climb. But now I wondered how high the climb would be in a Jewish house. I thought of the coming hazing rituals, or house initiation. I hoped I wouldn't become the only circumcised Chinaman in the state of New York.

SAILORS TAKE WARNING

HE ASKED ME to go sailing with him, just as I would ask a girl for a date. It wasn't just the words, but the way he looked at me. I felt a fleeting discomfort, and I dismissed it. Dismissing unpleasantries was a foible of mine, besides I'd never been sailing on the lake.

I liked Jack McInnis. I first met him at the start of school last year when I lived in the fraternity house. I didn't have a car and he'd go out of his way to offer me rides to campus. I accepted his friendship as a matter of course from a brother.

That September, summer persisted with cicadas buzzing in the elm trees and the warm southwesterlies coasting into the evening. We'd just finished dinner and Jack was giving me a lift to my apartment in his new '68 Jaguar. He had the top down and the air scuffled my hair as he shifted into third. I adjusted the headrest and looked up at the sky, and with a deep breath closed my eyes. Jack first brought up the weekend forecast, and then he asked me about sailing.

"How about asking a few of the other guys to go sailing with us?" I asked.

"No, I don't like a big crew, Grady," he said, his eyes on the road. "I'll pick you up nine sharp Saturday. We'll go all the way up the lake and back. We can make it a two-day trip."

In grade school we made fun of them and used words like homo and queer. They were abnormal, it was said. Paul and Paula Rawlings were twins in Mrs. Berry's class. Both tall and blond, they looked alike. But Paula had a bigger frame with broader shoulders and thicker muscles. Paul was fragile and demure. When we played kickball during recess, it was Paula whom everyone wanted on their team. She could boot the ball a mile high, but Paul didn't want to play, afraid he'd get hurt. We'd whispered about Paul. Sissy, we called him and I remember asking if he was a homo. Like the others I wasn't sure.

Some of us definitely knew Jimmy Allen was a homo. Jimmy had willingly used his mouth on several boys in restroom stalls. The story spread quickly but no one knew quite how to respond. We whispered and giggled, told jokes. If the school staff also had gotten wind of it, no action was ever taken. One day after school, my friend Robby and I detoured to our local drug store for a Popsicle. We took a short cut through the back of the shopping center, and behind the waste dump containers we saw a handful of boys in a brawl. Robby wanted to turn around, but I convinced him we could watch unnoticed behind a parked truck. Closer to the commotion I saw it wasn't a brawl, and I recognized Stanley Mitchell, the school bully who had a flat-top and the only kid with acne in our fifth-grade class. Everyone dreaded Stanley, who moved fearlessly with his gang. He had been expelled from school several times, which only emboldened him. Three others stood and watched. A boy was on his knees, head bent to the lot's blacktop, screaming and pleading with his hands covering his head. Stanley was swinging a stick at him as if it were a baseball bat. With one hand shielding his head, the screaming boy looked up, his face covered with blood. It was Jimmy Allen. Stanley gave a final kick to Jimmy's face, and his head flew back onto the coarse asphalt. When the mob left, Jimmy stood up, moaning and still writhing in pain.

I felt like a coward. I was a coward. We didn't go to Jimmy to see if he was okay, and afterwards Robby and I never talked about the incident. As far as I knew, Jimmy had never offended Stanley, and they didn't even know each other, but Stanley must have heard about the bathroom incident. Still, what was it to Stanley?

In 1965 the summer before college, I had had an encounter of sorts when I was returning to the States from Athens after a visit with my father, an embassy bureaucrat. I managed a three day stay-over in Rome, and to squeeze everything in I took the tourist route to the Vatican, the Sistine Chapel, and the Coliseum.

Late in the afternoon on the second day, I stood on top of the Spanish Steps overlooking the city. Men were scattered below, some seated and others traversing the incline. Against the orange sky, St. Peter's dome rose above the horizon. Next to me stood a tall man, lanky, middle-aged, wearing a tan suit. His perfectly trimmed hair was blond, not dirty blond but yellow like those you see in magazine drawings. He may have been a Scandinavian, German perhaps. He would glance at me and then quickly shift his stare to the city below. His eyes were cold blue and piercing, like a sea captain's in a novel. I looked at him and smiled, curious.

An Alfa Romeo zipped to the curve, stopping abruptly. The driver looked Italian—spectacled, balding and rotund. He got out and stood next to me looking at the view. "Beautiful."

"Yes it is," I said.

"You a American, *si*?"

"How did you know?" I said, grinning.

"Your a clothes, your a shoes, your a hair."

"It was that easy?"

"You a like to see city in my car?" he asked, pointing to his convertible.

"Yeah, sure." It could be a nice change from walking.

He shifted gears smoothly, and the Alfa Romeo sped around the Roman hill like a pinball shooting around the tracks. He looked at me and I looked back.

"I like to ask a question to you," he said. "Do you like a man?"

I didn't get it. "Yes, I like mankind."

"No, no. I mean a you like a man?" he said, cupping his stubby hands on my knee.

Suddenly my faced flushed and stomach tightened. I felt trapped but I remained calm. "No, I don't like," I said, mimicking his broken English.

"Why?" he said.

"Because I like girls," I blurted.

He drove his car back up the hill. It was as if he made a mistake, and he accepted it. He remained quiet and inexpressive until we reached our origin.

"I like a girl, too," he said. "But I like a man—for variety, for variety. Ciao."

As I watched Jack push the gearshift, I thought of how Jack's expression, and the German's, and the Italian's, were all the same. And maybe that was why I became uncomfortable when Jack asked me to go sailing. The look was not easy to describe—anticipation, apprehension, wistfulness.

Jack was not your typical second year law student. He was active in the fraternity when no other graduate student socialized in the house. No one knew when he studied; law students usually buried themselves in the stacks, but Jack was often seen lolling around the house. And, he was rich. That in itself wasn't unusual, but he was conspicuous; he had a 24-foot sailboat on the lake, a black Jaguar convertible, and always a wad of hundred dollar bills in his wallet.

Jack had gone to Columbia as an undergrad, where he'd been a member of our fraternity. He showed up one day at the house and declared himself a Beta chapter member. Fraters saw him as a die-hard fraternity member, a lifer. Besides, Jack was conversant in almost any topic and also a master chess player, bridge player, and guitarist. He never discussed law.

He had told me he was born during the war and never knew his father, who was buried in France. His father's family had owned a large shoe store chain in the city—half of the eight million people in Manhattan purchased their footwear from McInnis Shoes. Jack and his mother had lived in a two-level co-op near Central Park in the Upper East Side, and she had enrolled him in all the right schools. A uniform-ed chauffeur was always on duty. In summers Jack attended camps in the Adirondacks where his mother followed him and waited in the big hotels.

At twenty four Jack was already stout from too much beer and too many French fries. He had dark curly hair, long eyelashes and plump lips, the upper one coming to a point like a sparrow's beak. He wore Brooks Brothers shirts, usually under cashmeres, and never a tie, but he often wore an ascot.

Earlier in the month Jack had invited me to his apartment, a grand 19th century Victorian brownstone in town. The landlord, a Mrs. Greenwood, lived on the main floor and the two upper floors were modified into four separate units. Intricate woodwork framed the lead-lined windows and the walls were all walnut-paneled.

"Mrs. Greenwood doesn't allow any women visitors here, Grady," he had told me, looking away. His comment seemed out of place to me. While people described Jack as affable, I sensed he held back, like a fortune teller.

THE PREVIOUS YEAR, when I'd moved into the fraternity house, my assigned roommate had flunked out after his freshman year. I had the room to myself for the first few months, and Jack had often come up after dinner, sat on the empty bed smoking and telling stories. Thinking back, we had some laughs together then, and I remember I often looked forward to his company. When the next semester began, I was assigned a new roommate.

"Grady, I don't quite understand. Jack's throwing a cold shoulder at me," my roommate Gary had said shortly after moving in. "I don't think I've offended him in any way."

Jack was frustrated, I reasoned, because we couldn't have our usual time together after dinner, and he held that against Gary.

That Friday, Jack called to tell me a low pressure system from the south was moving in. "Grady, there are possible thunderstorms on Sunday," he said. "We'd better just make it an all-day Saturday outing. It should be a good sailing day—sunny, with light breeze. In fact, why don't we get an earlier start and I'll pick you up at seven."

All the better, I thought. I had exams coming up. Also, I had pondered the boat trip during the week, and the thought of sleeping on a tight sailboat with Jack made me uneasy. Then, I would discard my thoughts as unfounded or unfair to him.

Saturday morning Jack was in his form. He had his pilot shades on, top down on the convertible, and was wearing his ascot. We bolted into the A&P lot to pick up meats, beer and ice; Jack was humming as he shuffled down the store's aisles, giving me orders to pick up this and that. Back in the car, he was brandishing his knowledge of wind indicators—flapping of flags, grass movements along the road, and even waving patterns of women's dresses. Jack was excited.

The boat was docked in the town's marina where Jack had a year-round slip. The sails were tightly sheathed, and the deck was immaculate with perfectly wound ropes. Jack was right, a perfect sailing day, the bright morning light shimmering across the quavering water.

Jack had been sailing all his life on the Long Island Sound, where he kept a 42-foot Columbia. His movements on the boat were never jerky or quick, but rhythmic and deliberate like a seasoned pianist. He maneuvered the boat straight up the lake, and when the sails caught the westerly, we moved as if we were on a free-fall.

Jack opened the beer cans and he slurped the foam, the

wind stealing some. A gust bore heavily against my face, and I held a fixed smile to contain my exhilaration. The beer moved easily down my throat. We had beer for breakfast and lunch and ate salami pasted with mustard. In the afternoon I took off my sweatshirt when the temperature climbed, unusually high for the month. When the beer was nearly gone, I dozed off, lying flat on my back in the cockpit.

The sun was low when a chilled breeze woke me, goose bumps on my arms and chest. I slowly opened my eyes and turned my head to find my bearings. Seated behind the helm, Jack was studying me. The boat glided slowly and the air seemed muffled, accentuating our isolation—all of which made his stare more uncomfortable for me.

"Where the hell's my sweatshirt?" I finally said.

"You were out for awhile, Grady. We're getting to the marina now."

On the way home Jack was more subdued, and neither of us said much. I had recurring images of him staring at me in the cockpit and wondered what went through him.

LATER IN THE fall some of us were in the house living room drinking, and others were tubing. A group was hunched over a poker table. Jack strummed his guitar and sang a schmaltzy song he'd written about a farm boy and his dog. When he finished, people stopped to clap and asked for more.

The evening stretched out and someone made a comment about drinking beer on a weekend night without dates. We weren't tanked but we were loud, and I claimed I could get a blind date with any freshman out of the Pig Book—the photo manual of freshman names, with residence and phone number. Jack liked my grandstanding and joined in.

"I'll make you a deal, Grady," he said. "If you can get a date from a coed that we select from the book, I'll chauffer your date."

"Why would I want you to chauffeur us?" I asked.

People stopped chattering to hear our volley.

"Because I'll chauffer you in a 1941 Packard 180. Because I'll have chauffeur's uniform, including a cap."

"A 1941 Packard 180?"

"Yeah. It looks new. I have it stored in the city, and I'll go get it if you win the bet."

Jack and the others combed the Pig Book and selected a Kristin Ainslee—Wilkes Barre, Pennsylvania; government major; Balch Hall. No one knew her but they agreed on her photo—blonde, tall from the length of her neck, and probably bitchy. She was a perfect candidate. They were thinking that all her weekends were booked 'til spring break. Actually, I was thinking that also.

The phone on the coffee table was placed in front of me, and all waited to see me get shot down. More beer was passed. Jack was hamming it up for the larger audience, and he put down his beer and grabbed his guitar. "*I'm back in the saddle again...*" Texas accent and all. Others joined him.

I was trapped, but all the same I figured I had a shot. Co-eds accepted blind dates all the time. I thought about this Kristin, a freshman from the sticks. And the good-looking ones, the intimidating ones, don't get asked out, I told myself. Probably never been anywhere beyond Scranton.

When I dialed her number, I was told to wait. That upped my confidence a bit—Friday evening, and she was in her dorm. Kristin finally picked up the phone, her voice tenuous.

I jumped straight to the point. "Kristin, my name is Grady Talbot and the truth is I'd like to ask you out. The guys in my fraternity and I were discussing campus dating, and the co-eds having a three to one ratio advantage—well, the guys were complaining the coeds were snootier than coeds in other schools. I told them that just wasn't the case."

There was silence, and then she began to giggle.

"I'm not kidding," I continued. "They actually went through the Pig Book, and selected you as a test case—the most attractive coed in the book."

The giggling turned to laughter. Loud laughter.

"They dared me to call you to make a date. So, I'm asking you to go out with me next week. I'm a third year government major myself, and I can at least fill you in on the courses to take and avoid."

The laughter stopped. "Well, what do you have in mind?" she asked.

"Saturday, we could flick out. *2001* is playing downtown and I'll pick you up at six. Then we can get something to eat in Collegetown."

"I'm in Balch," she said.

"I'll see you at six on Saturday," I told her.

All focused on me as I hung up, silent. Jack was silent also.

He finally spoke. "Well, I'll leave for the city tomorrow to get the Packard."

Jack did as he said, went to the city, and when he returned, he drove up to the front of the house and honked a distinctive blaring horn. House members came out for the show. The Packard looked as if it had rolled out of Detroit yesterday—dark cobalt blue, white walled wheels with a red inner lining, massive chrome grill with matching fenders. Jack said the 8-cylinder, 186 horsepower engine powered the car's 4,000-pound body. The detailing was lush with thick burgundy carpets and soft leather. The paint reflected the dark trees against the sallow sky.

On Saturday Jack donned an old fashioned chauffeur's uniform—black tie, black Florsheim shoes, and a chauffeur cap. He even conveyed deference. It was as if he were rehearsing in a movie set, and I'm sure he had studied his chauffeur for years.

I sat in the back as Jack drove to Balch Hall. His back sat stiff and straight, his gloved hands gently turning the mahogany wheel. Jack had insisted I also play the part, and so I was in a three-piece suit—subtle pinstriped Gabardine wool. A suit wasn't out of place in Balch on Saturday nights.

"I'll get the door, sir," he said as he parked. He got out, opened the door, and stood at attention. Coeds looked out the dorm windows, gaping at the limo and the chauffeur swabbing the hood with a plumed duster.

Kristin stepped down the stairs, graceful like a dancer. She wore a neatly pressed dress with little lavender flowers. She was every bit as pretty as her photo. She extended her hand and smiled.

"Have you heard about the limo outside?" she asked, her voice delicate. "The girls are saying someone has a date with royalty."

When I told her the limo was mine, her smile disappeared. She looked me over, her eyes shifting rapidly. As we walked, she pressed her dress with her hands.

Jack opened the door, stoic. The ride to the theater was only fifteen minutes, and I made small talk of the government department and the faculty members. She was only partially attentive, as she studied the car's upholstery, chromed ornaments, and mahogany panels lining the doors. She had a faint smell of lilacs.

Kristin discretely scrutinized Jack as well. Jack didn't utter a word during the trip. He and I made eye contact through the rear view mirror, but I couldn't read his thoughts.

"I'll be waiting for you at 8:45, Mr. Talbot," Jack announced, opening the car door.

"That'll be fine, Jack," I said.

Kristin seemed to be taken in by the movie, but she did glance at me occasionally, probably wondering to which robber baron family I belonged. On screen, HAL, the mad computer, played a game of chess with one of the astronauts. I turned to Kristin and whispered the truth about my masquerade into her ear, and she chuckled loudly enough to annoy the people in front of us.

Jack picked us up in front of the theater, and then drove us to Johnny's Restaurant in Collegetown. Kristin was relaxed and quick to smile. When she laughed, she tilted her head back, as if to look at the ceiling.

She told me her family had been in the Scranton-Wilkes Barre area for almost 200 years. Her father was a Hopkins-educated pediatrician, who had returned to his hometown. She said she also would return after school.

"What's in Wilkes Barre?" I asked. "It's got coal and cold weather."

Kristin laughed again. Her mouth was on the small side, slightly turned down at the ends, and didn't quite fit her face. Her forehead was as broad as her eyes were large, making her appear to be steadily smiling. Her height only exaggerated her delicate build, and I imagined her chest had not changed much since puberty. She combed her blonde hair parted on one side with a brown clip on the other.

She told me she had been to a few fraternity parties, and she'd dated several upperclassmen but also took her studies seriously and used the weekends to book. The weekends had fewer distractions in the dorms, she said. Lucky for me.

Kristin only mentioned Jack to say that he must be a very good friend to spend a Saturday evening like this, even as a prank. "He played his role so well," she said. I didn't tell her he was the real robber baron.

We began to see each other regularly and by spring exclusively. She became familiar with the brothers, and at date-night dinners, Jack often sat with us. They became friends.

After spring weekend I was having lunch with her on campus. She was buoyant, recalling the events. It had been her first fraternity weekend party—a 48-hour, non-stop bash of banquets, dances, champagne brunches, lawn parties, and black tie dinners. Then she made an unexpected remark.

"Grady, I don't think Jack likes me," she said.

"What do you mean?"

"He doesn't like me. He puts on a nice front, but I sense resentment. On the other hand, when he looks at you, he lights up."

"What?" I said, my voice rising. "You're imagining things."

"No, Grady, I don't think so. I've seen him change, quite suddenly when he sees you. He's like a peacock opening his feathers."

I didn't like the reference and became silent—an angry silence that she sensed. She was implying Jack was in love with me. But so what? Why did I suddenly feel angry? She wasn't being accusatory. Gary had said the same thing, and if Gary had made a peacock reference, I don't think I would have been angry. But it was different with her.

And was Jack in love with me? I could ask him, but to what end. If he wasn't gay, it would only hurt him and damage our friendship, and even if he were, he might not admit it...or if he did admit, I thought only embarrassment could result.

I didn't see Kristin for the next few days as I continued to mull over what she had said. I couldn't discard it or bury it. Jack came to the house for dinner and later asked me if I wanted a ride to my apartment. We ended up at the Alt

Heidelberg, a student hangout in Collegetown, and also where Jack spent more time than the law library.

"Jack, are you gay?" I asked after a long chug of my beer. I had toyed with a hundred different ways to ask this question, but there was no easy approach.

He stared at his mug and then swished his beer as if the answer was lost in it. "Grady," he said without looking up. "I'm what they call a bisexual."

"Have you ever been with a woman?"

"No."

I wanted to pursue his answer but decided against it. His response may have been a defensive one, or his way of easing the revelation. I wasn't sure. I almost said I wasn't gay, but that would have been defensive and possibly insulting.

He drank more beer and then started on a long discourse about his first encounter at a camp in the Adirondacks when he was thirteen, his clandestine affairs at Columbia, and living with his secret. As he continued, I could see he was becoming more comfortable and relieved. But when our eyes met, I saw a glint of despondence, perhaps knowing our relationship would change.

Afterwards, when we saw each other, he was still pleasant but distant. At the house he would mingle with others, eat at a different table, and slip away from the house without a goodbye. I didn't fully understand his new behavior, or why, but it wasn't necessary for me to tell him his secret would remain so.

I cooked dinner for Kristin in my apartment later that

week, chicken legs and white rice. I even found a clean table-cloth for the table. I avoided the topic of Jack and I sensed she was in agreement.

Like other evenings in my apartment, we studied after dinner, Kristin reading on my bed and me at my desk. I stopped typing to look at her. She was on her side, lost in her book. Her fingers combed her hair, strands freed from the clip. She looked up and smiled. I went to her and wrapped my arms around her and kissed her. Images of Jack appeared, like a tune in my head that refused to leave.

STUCK ON RACHEL

IF YOU WERE from Kentucky, on scholarship, and Jewish, why would you want to join a fraternity full of New York and Lon-gh G-island Jews, mostly wealthy, with accents worse than yours? That's what I had to ask myself before I joined Alpha Epsilon in my freshman year. When I told my father, a hardware store owner in Lexington, that I had pledged a house full of New York Jews, he said, "Better you than me,

David."

It's not that I had anything against these guys from the city—meaning New York City—it's just that I never knew anything about them, though I had been warned by my father. By the end of my freshman year, I realized they had nothing in common with my Kentucky friends back home. There weren't too many Jews in Kentucky back in the Sixties, though we were only sixty miles from Cincinnati, and there were two temples somewhere in the city, though I don't know their whereabouts even to this day. The only Jews my parents knew were my Aunt Miriam and Uncle Stu, who'd come for dinner during Passover.

To someone like me, these New Yorkers could appear to be loud and obnoxious, often mixing Yiddish into their chatter. On the other hand, I started to see another side of them living in the frat house in my sophomore year. They were focused and serious, certainly more than the people back home and more than the rest of the campus. The upper classmen were editors of the newspaper, managers of the literary magazine, and the more respected members of the debate team. Unlike me, they would read the *Times* editorial pages and book reviews, discarding the sports section.

I was a novelty to them, like Lenny Kaplan who was in ROTC. But it wasn't long before they became used to my unfamiliar accent and manners, and at the same time I made an effort to learn Yiddish and tone down my Kentucky drawl. I also worked as many hours as I could handle in the kitchen, which eased my finances.

Early in that school year, Bob Gorman and I were in the kitchen sorting flatware, kibitzing with Harry. Harry never understood it, but whenever he said, "Why, everybody know Hay-reh Bay-reh in Fer-lor-reh-dah," we all cracked up. The house loved the cook, a large black man with a wide smile and gold-capped teeth. A week didn't go by when he didn't mention his younger days, back when Harry had been a singer and dancer with a local band in Miami.

"You boys'll be in the synagogue this Friday, ain't you?" Harry said, chopping the vegetables. "Yom Kippur's coming up."

"I think the last time I was in a temple was Yom Kippur—over ten years ago," I said. "I forget why now. Shoot, my mother must have told me a few times."

"Christ, Wolfson, you really are a redneck; it's the Day of Atonement," Bob said, not looking up from his forks and knives.

Everyone called me Wolfson. I guessed they had trouble calling a redneck *David*.

"Atonement for what, Bob?"

"For all the sins against God during the past year. You're to demonstrate your repentance and make amends."

"But it ain't for sins against a person," Harry said. "You gotta deal directly with that person for that."

"And reconcile before Yom Kippur," Bob added. "And no eating and drinking, no bathing, no sex, and no wearing leather shoes."

No wearing leather shoes? I'd never heard about that part.

103

Jesus, I was thinking even Harry knew more than I did.

"You know, I can take the fastin' and no bathin' part, but no sex? That's a bit much."

"Wolfson, when was the last time you got laid on Yom Kippur?"

Only a handful of the house members actually went to the synagogue on Yom Kippur, and I didn't see any people with tennis shoes that day. But I was sure nobody had sex on Yom Kippur.

House members gathered for dinner at the house each night, though the dinner staff ate earlier. I had the weekday shift and the work wasn't bad, taking up a couple of hours a day. Saturday dinners were different. Jackets and ties were required and it was guest night. As rituals go it was important. Bringing coeds to dinner was a status measurement of sorts, a feather in your cap—the prettier the coed or the more coeds you brought, the bigger and more numerous the feathers. But there were other kinds of feathers to be won. There was after-dinner entertainment during dessert, and sooner or later everyone was required to perform. Many loved performing, often competing with one another. A few danced to music and one or two sang, but most had a shtick—a standup comedy, a joke, or something amusing. That was another thing—if anything was unfamiliar to me, it was New York Jewish humor—far removed from Kentucky. But I liked their sarcasm, and I was beginning to take to it.

Everyone had waited for the redneck—what few of the fraters called me—to perform. I couldn't get out of it and I agonized for days before my turn.

Mickey Goldberg, my big brother and a wise-guy Brookly-ite, came through. "Wolfson, for you, make it short and watch your timing." And then he proceeded to give me my lines and some performance tips.

I was ready on a date-night. The spotlight was on. I stood on the floor, the brothers and their dates anticipating.

I paused for a good two seconds, searched the audience, and looked dumb. "Until I joined this here house," I started in a Kentucky rhythm, "I thought a *genital* was a non-Jewish person."

The audience cracked up, the dates as well. While some were on the floor, I continued. "Not only that, I thought *urine* was the opposite of *you're out.*"

I paused while the laughter slowly ceased—completely. In silence, I paused again looking squarely at them. "And I be-lieved an *enema* was someone who wasn't no friend."

The routine lasted less than a minute, but after that every-one took me for a long lost brother.

JEFF LOEB AND I had decided to be roomies in the house during pledging. We knew each other in freshman year as chemistry majors, but Jeff's life ambition was to become a medical doctor, which was counter to Jeff's history. His father, his grandfather, and his great grandfather had all been well-known New York City rabbis.

He'd grown up in New Rochelle in affluent Westchester County, and he'd had it easy. His family was well off, though he poked fun at his father. "He carries a Lipton tea bag in his wallet, and in restaurants, even the expensive ones, he'll ask for hot water, just to save fifteen cents," Jeff had told me. But Isaac, his father, was a gentle soul who thought well of everyone. Of the Irish, he would say, "They're okay, they're okay in my book." The Chinese were "of an ancient and learned culture and you've got to respect them," and even the Arabs were "our brothers."

I had met Jeff's parents at the beginning of the year. His mother, Esther, barely five feet and stringy, was the practical one. "Medicine is a noble profession, Isadore," she would say to him. She was a good Jewish mother, looking out for her family, and she managed to get things her way. When Jeff had returned to school after Thanksgiving, he called his mother long distance. The operator said, "This is a collect call from Jeff, will you accept?" And the mother would say, "No, I will not," and hang up. Jeff had safely reached school and she would save 55 cents. She was a product of the Great Depression, when saving change was as automatic as breathing.

Our room in the fraternity house was large and paneled in light oak. A picture window covered the west side looking down on the town through thick foliage, mostly hemlocks and pines. We had been sitting at our desks in silence glued to our books for almost an hour, our backs facing each other, the afternoon sun flushing the room with uncomfortable warmth.

I took off my sweater and broke the silence. "Hey, Jeff, you gonna be goin' to the party on Saturday?"

"I don't know. I was thinking about tooling at the library," Jeff said, turning to face me. Jeff's favorite word, tooling. When he said tooling, he meant booking—booking nonstop.

"It's a Saturday, boy. Why are you paying all them social dues? Jesus, give yourself a break."

"Maybe I'll get back to the house by eleven. The party should be going by then."

To some, Jeff might have come across as a nebbish, one of my acquired Yiddish words meaning an innocuous and timid person; he wasn't, but at times he came close. On the other hand, girls turned to look at him—dark hair, straight nose, symmetrical eyebrows, and chiseled features. Girls told him he looked like Adonis, Jeff claimed, and he'd mention that when someone called him a tool. During Spring Weekend freshman year, I had met his girlfriend Eileen, a doe-eyed sweet thing that every son's mother would love. She and Jeff couldn't take their eyes off each other, and it was nauseating. But you couldn't help liking her. As soon as they finished college, she would become Mrs. Eileen Loeb.

Still, Jeff did like looking at the coeds, and he liked talking about them: "Jesus, so and so is such a piece" or "what I'd do for an hour with her in bed." But it was all talk. For him Eileen was the only girl. They had sworn to each other to save themselves for their honeymoon, and they had both remained virgins. Jeff's pledge to Eileen was important in another way: It gave him stability. He didn't spend all his time looking for someone, gaping and wasting time at the student union and Collegetown bars like the rest of us. He stuck to his schedule, and he wouldn't allow women, or anything else, to interfere with his defined path to a medical career. No way I could follow such a regimen. Hormones. Coeds—they were latched to our cortex. I thought if I had a permanent woman, or even got married, my schoolwork would be a snap, a lot easier anyway.

THE SATURDAY PARTY was an annual event with Lambda Phi, our unofficial sister house. Some of the guys complained that the sorority was a full of cute yentas, but a lot of the Alpha Eps dated them, and in the past a few brothers had married them.

At dinner the brothers talked of getting lucky or herding one into a room—mostly wishful thinking, considering the girls' track record—even more so, the guys.

"Does anyone know if Bonnie Myerson's coming tonight?" I heard someone ask.

"Doesn't matter. She's going with some turkey at Tau Delta now. Even if she comes, there's no chance."

"Hey, Klingman, if I'm getting *shtupped*, you might have to sleep in the living room."

"What about the new pledges? I heard there are some real pieces in the class."

"Hey, I heard there are a couple of shiksas now."

After dinner the tables and chairs were moved out to the walk-out patio, and the band, a group called the Royals from Syracuse, began to set up the instruments in the corner of the dining room. Large bowls, with fruit punch spiked with vodka, were placed on tables.

"Where are the beer kegs?" I asked.

"Wolfson, Jews don't drink beer," Larry Binder said. "We only drink J&B. That's Jewish Booze. Besides, after drinking the punch, you're not gonna want beer. The stuff'll get you plastered instantly."

The band started out with the Kinks' "You Really Got Me." The sisters showed up, and the floor started to bounce. There must have been 50 people jerking and swaying like tranced tribal dancers in some ritual. The punch bowl drained quickly, and when "Louie" played, there wasn't anyone who wasn't on the floor, not even the house nebbishes—no one held back. The room became muggy, the punch gone again, and people demanded straight scotches and vodka.

She was shaped more like a woman than a coed, and she approached me tending the bar. The way she shifted her hips cut into me. "Hey cutie," she said. "You look like you can use a break." And she grappled me onto the dance floor.

Her name was Rachel Wilkinson from a little town outside of Pittsburgh. She had no inhibitions, and half the time she had her eyes closed as if she were dancing with herself. I had been watching her as she had moved from one guy to the next, while drinking like someone who just finished parole.

"What's your name?" she asked when the music slowed to a finish.

"David, but people here call me Wolfson."

"David, you don't look Jewish," she said.

"I'm Jewish." I reached for my zipper.

She let out a giggle. "I already heard about you—the Jewish redneck."

We walked upstairs to the living room, and as soon as we sat on one of the sofas, I feigned passing out and lowered my head on her shoulder. She was laughing now, and she placed her hand on my cheeks as if I were a child.

Marshall Kirsch, a senior from Long Beach, was roaring drunk, staggering from group to group trying to be amusing. When he saw me with Rachel, he wobbled over giggling and said, "Look." And he unzipped his fly, showing his flaccid state.

"Put that silly thing away," Rachel said casually.

I was impressed. She was composed and so cool, even though she'd been drinking all evening. I was in love. She was a knockout, and I was just about to let everything go and jump her—she knew it and was waiting for me.

Then Jeff appeared, like a traffic cop, out of nowhere. "Hey, Wolfson, what's going on?" he said, eyeing only Rachel.

"You're missin' a good party, boy," I told him, a little miffed. "Ah, this is Rachel."

Their eyes latched like two magnets of opposite polarity. I was jealous and ticked off. Just as I'd hoped, I finally met a willing coed who'd save me.

"Rachel, this is my roommate, Jeff. And he's Jewish," I said. It just came out that way—what a schmuck I am, I thought.

"Hello, Jeff, who's Jewish," Rachel said not taking her eyes off of him.

Son of a bitch didn't even acknowledge me. It didn't even occur to him I was with her, and he probably assumed Rachel was one of those Nordic Jews because he immediately invited her. "You wanna help me get some punch?"

"You don't mind, do you, David?" she said getting up. They left together.

Why should I mind, I asked myself. I was about to get laid, and *poof*, it all vanishes when Jeff appears, like a pitcher putting out 26 straight players toward a perfect ball game and then the last batter knocks the ball out of the park. I sat on the sofa feeling like a schlimazel. I looked around the darkened living room, people paired and busy with their partners. I stood up and went downstairs to the dance floor.

They were slow dancing to *Smoke Gets in Your Eyes*, real slow. Rachel had her head on his chest, and Jeff had his eyes closed. I hoped the bastard was thinking of his Eileen. I was feeling my vodka, drowsy and tired, and I went back up to the living room and passed out on the sofa.

The vodka interrupted my unquiet slumber. It was four o'clock when I went down the hall to relieve myself and then I slogged to my room. When I turned the door knob, it was locked. Even in my state I knew Jeff was in the room with Rachel. I was too dopey to make a fuss and I returned to my sofa in the living room, heavy smell of stale cigarettes lingering. There were a handful of people asleep on other sofas, including a few sorority sisters.

When I opened my eyes, it was ten in the morning, the living room awash in early light, the house calm and hushed.

Nearby some of the same people were still in a slumped state. When I entered our room, Jeff was already in front of his desk, booking no less.

The previous night seemed like a distant dream and Rachel was still in my thoughts, but now in the sunlight my excitement for her seemed imagined. Still, I remembered how I coveted her, how jealous I was, and how abashed I felt when Jeff took her away. But I wasn't going to let him know.

"All right boy, what happened?" I asked him.

Jeff put down his pencil, got up, and plunked down on his bed. Flat on his back, he stared at the ceiling as if he were in a shrink's office. "Wolfson, I've got tsores."

"What the hell you talkin' about?"

"I've got tsores, troubles," he said.

"So who doesn't? At least you got shtupped last night. Right?" I said studying him.

He just stared at the ceiling.

"All right, details," I said.

"Well, I drank a couple of those damn punches. Jesus, who the hell concocted the drinks? It was eighty percent alcohol. Anyway, I got pretty damned high, and she says, 'It's too stuffy in here. Let's get out to the patio.' And as soon as we get to the fresh air, she turns to me and attacks me—all over."

"Then what happened?" I asked, not looking at him.

"I got hot, that's what happened. She was like a wet dream, Wolfson. Unbelievably good looking. And Jesus, what a body! And you know something? She's smart as hell. She's a linguistics major—speaks three foreign languages."

"Jeff, did you do it or not? Get to it."

"Hold on. So, she sees how I'm going crazy over her, and she says we should go to my room. We didn't bother to even turn the lights on, just started to undress each other. Wolfson, it was unreal. Unreal!"

"All right, already. It was unreal."

"At this point, I'm aroused. I mean really aroused. She knew exactly what she was doing—stroking me and touching me in all the right places. And she knew how to use her tongue. Wolfson, it was unbelievable, I was going crazy! But I had the sense to go into your desk and get a Trojan, a lubed one."

"You had no problems putting it on in the dark?"

"It was weird. As I was putting the damn thing on, the strangest thing happened. I started to think about Eileen. It was like I couldn't get her face out of my mind. The harder I tried, the more vivid she became. Anyway, I looked at Rachel, lying there waiting for me. So, I pressed on and entered her, and she was lovin' it. I'm telling you, Wolfson, she was lovin' it."

"All right, she was lovin' it."

"Then something worse happened. An image of my mother appears, and I hear her asking me, 'What are you doing with a shiksa, Jeffrey? What about Eileen?' It was awful, and I began to shrivel up. I had to pull out. It was awful."

"Jesus, Jeff. And Rachel couldn't help you out?"

"She tried. And I tried. The more we tried, the worse it got. We just lay there and talked. She really didn't seem to mind, and we talked a good 45 minutes, and then we fell asleep. She got up several hours ago, dressed and left. Before leaving the room, she told me to call her later."

What's that German word? *Schadenfreude*. I was actually getting satisfaction from Jeff's story.

"So, what is this tsores thing you're talking about?"

"I think I'm in love, Wolfson. God, she's something else."

"Jeff, don't be ridiculous. And what about Eileen?" I couldn't help reminding him.

"That's the tsores. I'm confused."

"Are you gonna call Rachel?"

"I don't know. How am I going to face Eileen? I've got to tell her, I think. And, I've already lost my virginity. That's shot to hell. On the other hand, I can't stop thinking about her—Rachel, I mean."

Later that day I overheard Mike Winer chattering away about the party in the living room. "Jeff's the only one who scored at the party. And he didn't even get here until the party was almost over." To which George Baron added, "Yeah, did you see her? Rachel what's-her-name? She's not exactly miskayt." Miskayt meant ugly.

Jeff did call Rachel. And he continued to see her, but he wouldn't bring her over to the house. A few of the guys were from towns adjacent to his home in New Rochelle, and he didn't want to take any chances. They met often, in the evenings, afternoons and even during lunch. Sometimes they went to her sorority and also to his bomb, his car—a '59 Chevy Impala convertible with the outrageous bat wing fins. Jeff's schedule and his routine went out the window, and that was a problem. Without his schedule, Jeff's assignments, studies and even lecture attendance suffered—really suffered. The more he saw her, the more obsessed he became. And frazzled and depressed.

"I know I'm in trouble, Wolfson," Jeff said one evening after seeing Rachel. "I know my life's going to hell. She's like a bad addiction and I'm scared."

"How does she feel about you?" I asked.

"You know, I really can't say. Sometimes I think she's crazy about me, and at other times, my gut says she's just having fun with me. She's complicated. It's like she's not predictable."

"What are you going to tell Eileen when you see her next week?"

"I don't know," Jeff said biting his lower lip. "Are you sure you don't want to come and stay at my house? My mother makes good turkey."

Instead of leaving town for Thanksgiving, I decided to stay in the house. Flying to Kentucky was just too expensive, and besides classes were cancelled for only two days. "Thanks anyway. I'm behind in a couple of my courses."

"Couple of courses? I'm behind in all of mine. Wolfson, I'm scared shitless."

"Listen, Jeff. When you're down home, away from Rachel, take a good look at everything. See Eileen. And think about what you really want, and make up your mind one way or the other. The problem now is that everything's hanging in the air. And you...It's impossible for you to live that way."

Everything I told him was true. I just left out the part about me, and my interests.

"You're right," he said.

Two others didn't leave town for Thanksgiving: Jon Phillips, who didn't want to fly all the way to Los Angeles, and Al Palevsky, an engineering student who was on probation. During the break we saw rain every day, and when it ceased, the humidity was so high the air oozed tiny water drops. All three of us locked ourselves in our rooms during the day and didn't see each other, except when we broke for dinner.

For Thanksgiving, we drove to town to Joe's Restaurant, a handful of other customers keeping us company. "You know, the food was good, the company sucked," Al said smiling after dinner. Like I said, I was beginning to appreciate Jewish humor. Climbing back up East Hill on State Street the wet, glimmering brick pavement rattled the wheels, echoes bouncing off dark empty houses. We were in a ghost town.

When Jeff returned to the frat house late Sunday evening, the first words out of his mouth to me were, "It's all over!"

"What's all over?" I asked, hoping.

"Me and Rachel, that's what's all over," he said, unpacking his suitcase and arranging his clothes into drawers.

"Did you tell Eileen about Rachel?" I asked.

"Yeah. I did. I told her about Rachel, and she started to cry.

But I'll tell you something, Wolfson, when I saw her and I saw her cry, I never felt so bad in all my life. Right there, I knew it was over, it wasn't even close. I love Eileen. Right there, I made up my mind."

"Did you tell her you went to bed with Rachel or not?"

"Yeah. That's when she started to cry. I told her how sorry I was, and I told her it wouldn't ever happen again. She kept crying and wouldn't stop, and finally she ran home. Anyway, the next day she called me up to tell me she wanted to see me. When I went over to her house, she told me she had time to think things over, and then she asked me if I would stop seeing Rachel, for good. I told her I wouldn't see Rachel ever again. She hugged me and told me she loved me. I told you— it's all over."

"And you'll never see Rachel again?"

"I'll see her one more time to say goodbye. That's it. Look, Wolfson, she was like a bad fever. When I saw Eileen, the fever broke, and I think I'd definitely flunked out if things keep going. I swear all this was the damndest thing."

The very next day Jeff saw Rachel and did break off with her. When he told me, I thought of immediately of calling Rachel. But that would be too soon, I thought. I'd wait a week.

CAPTAIN KIRK'S GAMBIT

IN MY YOUTH, I had made a commitment to study science and mathematics, the language of numbers, but I learned early on that the usage and manipulation of words were far more powerful—powerful enough to saved my friend from a life-altering predicament.

The freshman year was coming to a close and everyone sensed the danger, the panic settling in. We'd been screwing off, procrastinating, and now it was dues time with cramming and all-nighters. Back then in 1966, there was only one Xerox machine in the student union building, and the lines were like the post office on tax day. There were even talks of gorging out—hurling yourself off the campus bridge—the school's distinctive path to an unceremonious departure.

I was finishing my physics project in my dorm, going blind pushing my K&E slide rule, aligning miniscule lines to miniscule lines. I hadn't used this expensive instrument in high school, and there were times I'd push it back and forth, back and forth—hypnotizing myself by the numbers moving in parallel. On their way to class, engineering students with crew cuts and pimples dangled their ivory sticks in leather scabbards like knights marching to battle.

Nigel walked in the door, doubled over laughing. "Bill, you won't believe what just happened."

I didn't look up from my desk. "Nigel, I need you to shut up. I'm trying to finish my damn physics project."

"The hall phone rings and Keller answers it," he said, dropping onto his bed. "The turkey says, 'Yeah, what the hell do you want?' and the caller says, 'I'd like to talk to Richard Rusk.'"

I threw my pencil on the desk and turned to him. "So?"

"So, Keller says 'The sonofabitch ain't here,' and the caller says, 'Tell the sonofabitch that the sonofabitch's father called.' Then he hung up."

"You're kidding?"

"No, it's the truth," he said shaking his head. "Bill, the Secretary of State actually said that. Can you believe that? Dean Rusk."

Still laughing, he reached for one of his Newports in his shirt pocket, sliding the cigarette over his ear, then took out another and placed it on one side of his lips. Nigel's lips were ever moist as if priming for his next cigarette. He was short and his cheeks looked like they'd been smeared with rouge. He was a Brit from Yorkshire but grew up in Pennsylvania. Except for his accent Nigel was as American as I was. The accent was an advantage, he'd said, not only with girls but with everyone, making him appear more intelligent and different.

In the first week of school, the campus radio station WVBR had hired him as a disc jockey for five days a week, eight to ten in the evening. The station liked his accent, and so did the audience. The problem, of course, was Nigel was placed on academic probation after the first semester. His prep school training was almost equivalent to freshman college level but wasn't enough for him to coast through the engineering curriculum; he didn't take his class assignments seriously either. He did, however, tutor many of us who were desperately struggling during the first semester, especially me.

His father had driven him up to school in September. The reserved and distant Englishman was a character out of a Victorian novel, gray hair and mustache, Herringbone jacket. His chin remained up, even when he sat. He said little, just a perfunctory hello and smile, a self-important smile one might find on a Viceroy of India.

Nigel spoke ill of no one except for his old man—bitter tirades at times, or ridiculing at other.

"He was so compulsive that if he had a meeting, he'd drive early enough to get to the appointment half an hour early," Nigel once said. "He'd then just wait in his car. Even for social occasions."

Nigel told me the only gentle moment with him was when he received his acceptance letter from the engineering school.

"Listen, I'm not quite done with Pudwell's project, and I want go to the chemistry review session," I said. "Have you finished yours? It's due at four, you know."

There was no response. He took a drag and stared at the ceiling. I didn't even bother to ask if he was interested in the review session.

"Look Nigel, have you finished yet?" I said, raising my voice. "The report represents a third of your grade. They'll throw you out if you can't cut 2.0 this semester; you'll be in 'Nam piloting a chopper."

"Actually, I'm about finished. Surprised you, didn't I?"

"Make sure you hand it in on time. It's due at exactly 4:00."

"Don't worry, I will." And then he was snoozing, leaving the lit cigarette burning in the ash tray.

That was his standard line, "Don't worry, I will."

It was close for Nigel. He frequently cut lectures and rarely studied. "Nigel," I had told him more than once. "You need to quit the radio station and buckle down."

"Don't worry," he always answered, the words coming out before I even finished my warning.

Nigel had one semester to pull up his grades, or they were going to bust him. But he continued to return to the dorms past midnight, finding a bullshit session, or even worse, a bridge game, and then not getting up until the next afternoon; other times, he'd be tubing out in the lounge watching *Star Trek*. By mid-semester he must have known he was in trouble. The draft boards were ready and waiting.

I left Nigel for the chemistry review. The TA, an East Indian, rambled about super-cooled liquids and bifurcation points, and I was lucky if I could pick up one in three words he uttered. I cut short the session to make sure my physics project was on time. All through the semester, Pudwell's class had a way of hovering and never leaving us.

Professor Elias Laren Pudwell taught freshman physics, a position of diminished status among the younger faculty. I hated lectures in Rockefeller Hall, not because of its architectural bleakness but because of Pudwell—a chubby, bespectacled, and balding man. Pudwell had earned his doctorate just before the war and joined thousands of other scientists to build the plutonium bomb. Like other physicists, he was determined to make breakthroughs and win a Nobel Prize. But he was a mere cogwheel in the project, crunching numbers and solving necessary but routine problems. No pure research for the professor, where quantum leaps and discoveries are made. Already in his thirties, he had returned to the university after the last bomb was dropped over Nagasaki. His door to breakthroughs and glory was shut. He had had a nervous breakdown during his tenure, and upon his return to teaching, he became creative and brought novelty to his classroom.

He demonstrated the Coriolis Effect by placing a heavy rotating gyroscope inside a suitcase and setting it on the lecture floor. A volunteer was asked to pick up the suitcase and walk straight across the lecture hall. Upon command, the student was told to make a sharp turn. As soon as he turned, the suitcase lifted itself into the air, pulling the student with it.

On a Lionel train, he built a tubular smoke stack encasing a spring-loaded missile with a mechanical triggering device—all to illustrate the Conservation of Momentum. As the train sped on its tracks, the missile, a pencil-shaped piece of wood, ejected straight up into the air just before it entered the tunnel. As the toy locomotive came out of the tunnel, the missile fell back into the smoke stack with precision. Students roared.

His most dramatic stagecraft was the demonstration of the pendulum. He attached a 30-pound iron ball to the ceiling by a slivery wire. The professor would pull the ball to his nose at one end of the hall, then close his eyes and release the massive spheroid. The ball would accelerate, pause for an instant at the other end of the hall, then charge back at the professor as if to pulverize his fragile head. But it would always stop a hair's width from his nose.

Almost always. One time, after years of performing this magic, the professor had moved his head forward, no more than a half inch, but just enough to break his nose and spatter blood on the wooden floor. He wore a large gauze around his nose for more than a month, a badge of his failure as a physicist.

I once walked into Pudwell's office without an appointment. He was sitting in his wooden chair and looking out his window—staring, clicking and re-clicking his ball point pen as if he were timing a falling object. When I asked him about a point in his lecture, he said, "Young man, I've no time to explain something so elementary. Go ask your TA."

I walked out sheepishly, and then I got angry. I'm paying all this tuition, including his salary, and he had the nerve to kick me out of his office?

I was thinking of Nigel when I submitted the term project to the Teaching Assistant. Sure, Nigel had said he finished the project, but he was napping on his bed when I left him.

I walked downstairs to the vending room for a cup of coffee and a smoke. A couple of students sat on a long bench table and one yelled out, "Bill, Did you get it in?"

"It's in," I said. "Just in time, too."

"You're probably the last submission," Tommy Petrone said. "Most people handed theirs in during the week."

We sat smoking our butts and talked mostly about Pudwell's exam scheduled for the next week.

"The only person who's going to ace the exam is Ingrid Nilsen," Dennis Kimmel said.

"Who's that?"

"You know, that quiet redhead, always at the back of lecture. Never says anything. You won't believe this, but she actually takes her physics exam with a fountain pen. Can you believe that? A fountain pen!"

"Jesus Christ, Mary and Joseph," Tommy blurted.

"Listen to this one. In the middle of last semester's final, she turns to me and says, 'Dennis, can you wake me up in about ten minutes?' She puts her head down on the desk and takes a nap. She aced the exam."

"She's actually a very nice person," I added. "If only Pudwell was."

"Right," Tommy said. "The damn Nazi is a sadistic bastard. Let me give you guys some advice. If you want to know what's on the exam, I'll tell you. It's what he covered on the last day before spring break when everyone skipped town. Then find out what he covered during Passover holidays when all the Jews were at temple. That's what'll be covered. He's a damned degenerate."

"Have either one of you guys seen Nigel?" I asked, breaking Tommy's rant.

They both shook their heads. Just then, Nigel appeared. We eyed him as he sat on the seat.

Dennis spoke first. "Nigel, you got your report in?"

"He wouldn't take it," Nigel said, shaking his head.

"Who wouldn't take it? What are you talking about?"

"I was fifteen minutes late. The Teaching Assistant wasn't in his room, so I went up to Pudwell's office to give him my report," Nigel said, pausing to stare at me. "He said it was too late." Nigel nodded, his face blank.

"So what's he going to give you on your report? An F?" Tommy asked.

"Yeah."

"Crap. You had a D on the mid-term," I said.

"That'll probably mean you'll flunk the course," Tommy added.

"Did you tell Pudwell that?" I asked.

"Yeah. He said I should learn to be punctual. 'A deadline is a deadline,' he told me. He didn't give a shit."

Nigel was upset, but not panicked. He got up and left.

"I told you Pudwell was a sadistic degenerate," Tommy said. "Something is wrong with him."

Dennis shook his head. "You know, Nigel's brilliant. Too bad he's such a fuckoff. He'll probably get drafted now."

Stepping out of Rockefeller, I was angry at Pudwell. He could have given Nigel the fifteen minutes, most professors would have. Instead, he had lectured Nigel. What's so critical about fifteen minutes, I asked myself.

And I was angry at Nigel. I didn't understand him. He knew his position and he could have easily come through; after all, he had finished the physics project. So it wasn't as if he had completely given up. Still, Nigel hadn't given up the radio station; he hadn't focused enough to make lectures; he hadn't bothered to turn in the project on time. It seemed as if he wanted to fail. But now, he was despondent—as despondent as I had been discouraged earlier in the year when I desperately needed help in my courses, when Nigel generously took time to coach me and guided me through. He was my roommate.

I turned and re-entered the building. I was going to have a talk with the professor—one chance in a hundred I gave myself of changing his mind, but I didn't care. I took the stairs to the second floor two at a time, then ran down the empty corridor to Pudwell's office. The hall seemed to echo. When I reached his door, he was reading a journal. I cleared my throat.

He looked up to say, "Yes?"

"Professor Pudwell, may I have a minute with you?"

"Sit down," he said, stone-faced.

"Professor Pudwell, I'm Nigel Lovell's friend, his roommate, actually."

"And who is Nigel Lovell?"

"Sir, Nigel tried to hand in his term project about fifteen minutes ago, and you refused."

"Ah yes. He was late. What's that to you? He already tried to make his case, and there was no case. So, good day to you."

"Sir, he's on probation. An F on his project will fail him in the course, and I think it will probably bust him out."

"He had already said that."

"Professor Pudwell, why is the fifteen minutes so important you'd fail him?"

"Son, this is not your business, and I think you should leave. Good day."

"Sir, with all due respect, you've been late and no one destroyed your life for it."

"Come again?"

"At the beginning of the semester I remember you were at least ten minutes late for a lecture."

He paused to think and then said, "Yes, that was the day we had an ice storm in the morning."

"You were late, sir, and no one fired you," I said, wondering if he was going to pull out a handgun and shoot me.

"What is your name, son?" he asked after a long pause.

"William Matson, sir."

"William, your roommate is lucky. Tell him to bring back his project."

I couldn't believe it, a hundred to one I had given myself. A hundred to one. I felt like a lawyer who convinced the Supreme Court to stave off an execution just before midnight. I remembered a *Star Trek* episode: A floating space probe—a computer the size of a golf bag—became aberrant from a technical malfunction. Its original mission was to decontaminate space colonies infected by a virus. But due to a glitch, the computer tried to get rid of imperfections everywhere—humans, in particular. Captain Kirk nabbed the computer onto his ship. At first the computer believed Captain Kirk was its creator, who had also been named Kirk, and the computer obeyed the Captain's commands; after all, if Kirk created the perfect computer, he must be perfect. Slowly, the computer caught on that Kirk was like others with human flaws and readies to destroy him and his crew.

The computer proclaims, "All imperfections must be destroyed, humans are imperfect, and therefore humans must be destroyed." At the last moment, Captain Kirk threw logic at the computer, telling it that it had made a mistake presupposing he, the captain, was its creator. Kirk convinced the computer another human named Kirk was the creator. The computer acceded to its mistake and obeys its own edict, and it destroyed itself. I remembered I laughed at Captain Kirk's self-satisfied look after he outwitted the computer, and now I'd checkmated that bastard Pudwell. I'd saved Nigel.

I hadn't expected Pudwell to destroy himself, but I was sure he would just kick me out like he did before. I had thought of him as an android—calculating, analytical, and logical. I wondered if Pudwell had ever loved a woman.

Outside the building I took a deep breath. I smelled spring, and I looked at the tall and graceful elms lining the street, swaying in an invisible breeze.

THE FOURTH CHIMP

ON MY EIGHTH birthday, my parents had taken me to the Baltimore Zoo where an episode left me skeptical about people all my life. The crowd gathered around a monkey cage, the late morning sun warming us just enough to take the chill out of the spring air. Three chimpanzees performed before the people, young and old donned in their best Sunday clothes, many with sunglasses. The three chimps worked hard, screeching while they somersaulted, pranced and flounced. I'd guessed then the chimps had learned their performance encouraged the spectators to throw peanuts, rewarding them for their exhausting act. After picking up the food and regaining their energy, the three chimps replayed their routine again—as taxing and wearisome as it was. There was a fourth chimp. Immediately after the threesome completed their show, and while they were consuming their gathered peanuts, the fourth chimp would jump in front of the gallery, execute a quick pirouette or two, and extend his begging hand to the admirers. The crowd laughed and then shoved their hands into paper bags to throw peanuts at the chimp—as many peanuts as before, perhaps more. And then the clever chimp would move aside and wait—wait for the trio to go back to work again.

There's a fourth chimp on every college campus. He's not an outstanding student, not a big-man-on-campus, and not a looker. But with little effort, he's able to turn everything he touches into money. I first met Kleivenstein when I joined a fraternity in the spring of my freshman year, though I'd heard stories about the upperclassman long before we shook hands. It was early September of '67 and I had returned to school a week early. I wanted solitude after months of frenzy and relatives in Baltimore, but mostly I wanted a head start finding a job. My uncle Chas traded in his car every three years like clockwork, and his Ford was due in December that year. He told me he'd give his '63 Falcon for $900. "The dealer would give me $1200 for it, but I'll let you have it for school."

A three-year-old car for under $1000, a deal I couldn't pass up.

I'd saved some money over the summer, but I fell short about $400 toward the car. Not having wheels in a fraternity house had its disadvantages, like being stuck on campus on weekends—a definite limitation with coeds. My father had told me money was tight, and a luxury like a car was up to me. A car for the coming year had been on my mind all summer.

Collegetown was strangely silent. The sun blazed, a dog followed a student, a couple blithely walked looking at windows, and store owners stood outside savoring the peace. I sat drinking coffee next to a picture window in Stuart's Bakery.

"Hey, Cort! Cort Ashby!" someone yelled through the panes.

It was Kleivenstein. I waved, then motioned him inside.

Though I asked him to sit, he stood next to my table scratching his ribs, obviously in a hurry—his normal state.

"Kleivenstein, you been here all summer?"

"Back and forth from the City. You know, I've got this laundry in Collegetown and a few other things. How about you?"

The City, meaning New York City. "I just blew in a few days ago, settling in before the rush."

"Listen, Cort, you interested in making some money before classes begin?"

"If it's legal, I'm interested."

Kleivenstein's face switched. "Look, I've got this distributorship for paper dresses. It's gonna be like the hula hoop."

"Paper dresses?"

"You'll make good money for little and easy work. Paper dresses are the next big thing. Talbot and Dodson are already on board, and we're gonna meet at the house."

"Paper dresses?"

"Listen, I haven't got time right now. I'll see you at the house Thursday. At five." He turned and yelled, "You in or what?"

"All right, see you the day after tomorrow."

His name really wasn't Kleivenstein but that was what everyone called him. Jon Rasmus Kleiven was his real name—not Jonathan, but Jon. He looked like a top, round in the middle, narrowing up his chest and down his legs. Close up, he wore glasses with black rims and darkened lenses, and at times they camouflaged the dark circles under his eyes. He had curly dark hair, short and thin, and cherubic cheeks like an angel in a seventeenth century Baroque painting. But he also had a schnoz. He was from Bay Ridge, a part of Brooklyn which was predominantly Norwegian with stingy smattering of Italians and Irish. For years the residents liked to point out that it was the only voting district in the city that went for Goldwater.

Christoffer Kleiven, Kleivenstein's father, was one of the square heads—as the Norwegians were called—who had immigrated to Brooklyn as a young man. He was hired with other Scandinavians to work the New York docks, but a ruptured disk in his lower back forced him to retire early, spending his days in anguish. On top of all this, his hearing had been dulled by years of hammering pile drivers. No one could make him wear a hearing aid.

As a kid Kleivenstein had sworn he would never work with his hands like his old man. Growing up near Fourth Avenue wasn't easy for Kleivenstein. A chubby sweet kid, he was an easy target. The tow-headed square heads made fun of his weight and his Jewish features, so they bastardized his name to Kleivenstein. Even after the tormentors realized Jon Kleiven was a Lutheran, the nickname stuck. It was always Kleivenstein and the name even became endearing to his friends. One of the upperclassmen in the house told me that in Kleivenstein's freshman year, everyone assumed he was Jewish, as did the fraternities. The Jewish fraternities rushed him but he pledged Delta Tau as a token Jew.

THE DELTA TAU house sat next to a gorge with a 200-foot drop. Not a stone mansion like many of the frat houses, the timber and glass structure stood sleek and functional, an example of Fifties architecture. In the fall the yellow and orange leaves reflected off the large windows, melding the house into the background.

Only Bill Johnson, the house manager, had beaten me to the house on Labor Day weekend, and soon others trickled in, including Mike Talbot and Avery Dodson, who had already agreed to work for Kleivenstein. Mike, an economics major, wanted a straight path to money, and he figured after his MBA the big trading houses would be knocking on his door. He considered law school, but that would be a year more, a year too long; "The forever optimist" was printed under his name in his Trenton High School yearbook. His exaggerated pug nose, pink and fleshy, and his pudgy build clashed with his hyper demeanor. His ever-blinking eyes were annoying and he moved as if he were a wound-up doll, except he never wound down.

Quite different from Mike, Avery Dodson was from Spartanburg, South Carolina, which had a population that wouldn't fill half of Yankee Stadium. Tall and lanky, Avery and Mike weighed the same and people called them Laurel and Hardy. Avery's movements were casual and deliberate, but his quick wit and his rustic sarcasm didn't fit his hillbilly accent. Nor did the shoulder length long hair which he grew over the summer; there were a few on campus who were looking like hippies, but it was a good bet he was the only one in Spartanburg. His father was an electrician, and at fourteen Avery tried to strip a wire using his teeth, forgetting the wire was live. The currents threw him across the room, which made him fall in love with electronics and study electrical engineering. His mother, a part-time vitamin salesman working from home, was so good on the phone that she made more money than Avery's father. She loved clichés: "It ain't a sale til the money's in your hand, hun" or "Let me tell ya somethin', honeychile, the time factor's everythin' in business."

With a view of water at the bottom of the gorge, Avery and Mike had a room which was bigger than the one I was to share with Alfred. They were rigging their elaborate stereo system when I walked in the door. Kleivenstein was Mike's big brother, so I assumed he and Avery had all the details. I wasn't totally right. Mike couldn't wait to start selling, but he didn't know much more than I did, only that the dresses were made of fire-resistant paper.

"So, how did Kleivenstein get the distributorship?" I asked.

"Who knows where the hell Kleivenstein latches onto things," Mike said. "The guy's unreal. He's into everything. Did you know he has two patents for bird feeders?"

"Bird feeders?" I asked, squinting.

Mike liked telling Kleivenstein stories. A couple of years ago Kleivenstein had been taking an ornithology class and was visiting Sapsucker Woods Bird Sanctuary by the airport. He saw people buying bird feeders—a lot of people—and the margins on the feeders were unreal. So he came up with a couple of designs of his own and patented them. Mike thought Kleivenstein was receiving a couple of hundred dollars a month in royalties from deals he had made with the manufacturers.

No one had ever seen Kleivenstein study and in fact no one knew his major, he'd changed it so many times. He saw opportunities everywhere. He had placed an ad in the Yellow Pages for AA Auto Service, and in the middle of winter when the whole town was buried under snow or when it was real cold, car batteries wouldn't work and people would call Kleivenstein's service thinking they were talking to the Triple A. His ad was just above the AAA in the book.

Kleivenstein hung out at the Collegetown Laundry. People on campus assumed he was just an employee, but Mike said he actually owned it. The rumor was Kleivenstein won the laundry from the town mayor in a private poker game with Chamber of Commerce members.

Avery stopped wiring and became serious. "Boys, I like Kleivenstein, and I'm happier than a dog with two peters about this paper dress thing. But I'll tell you somethin', that boy's slicker than a greased pig at a county fair. When we meet with him, I reckon we need to clear some things up before we get started."

I laughed. I loved the way Avery put his words together. "What do you mean, Avery?" I thought everything was set."

"Listen, Cort. This here's business. When you have an agreement, it's gotta be clear and plain as day—especially with our old boy Kleivenstein. That boy comes across smilin' and talkin' as sweet as my grandma's pecan pie, but he's wound tighter than a Gibson Guitar. And he ain't gonna give up nothin'. I do believe that boy wouldn't give up a nickel to see Jesus ridin' a bicycle."

We cracked up, but Mike became serious. "Come on, Avery, what are you trying to say?"

"Look, Mike (he pronounced it, Maack), first of all I ain't sure how many others Kleivenstein's already asked. I'll tell you one thing, if he'd already asked twenty people, I'm gone. It'll be a waste of time. Second of all, assuming we can get some kind of an agreement about the number of sellers, we need to talk about time frame. And by the way, we ought to ask for exclusivity."

"What the hell is that, Avery?" I asked again, feeling stupid.

"It means basically we'll be the only people who can sell these paper dresses—on campus, and maybe in town, and more important for some specified time duration. When we meet on Thursday, we really need to nail this thing down."

What Avery said made sense. Why wasn't I able to think like him? Was it encoded in his gene, or did someone coach him? My parents knew nothing about retail. My mother taught high school biology, and my father worked for the county. We had a modest but comfortable house in Towson, just outside the city. I had thought my father was aware of his moderate station in life. More than once I had heard him say, "We do things the right way, not like the others." The others meaning anyone who was not a White Anglo-Saxon Protestant. My father had once bought a radio that didn't work, and when I suggested an exchange at the store, he said, "I bought it, that's it." I'd thought my father was a fool. My mother was even worse, thinking bargaining was not proper.

My roommate Alfred finally arrived, two days late, while I was mowing the lawn. It was still summer, but the humidity was low, and I could smell fall—dried leaves with a hint of algae from the gorge. We'd first met in our history class the previous year, when he lent me his lecture notes after I had flu for over a week. He was proud of his home town, York, Pennsylvania, the home of York Barbell Company, as he proudly claimed; I never asked him whether that was the most important attraction in the city. He was a classics major, a nerd, really, but he was enthusiastic about everything, and it was contagious. When I filled him in about the paper dresses, he became as excited as Mike. "Whoa, you mean we'll get stinking rich before our junior year? When do we start?"

Kleivenstein walked into the house at exactly five o'clock. He didn't even say hello, the four salesmen waiting in the living room. Without sitting down, he launched into his talk.

"We're gonna make a bundle, it's not even close," he said. "There's a company in California that's selling 80,000 dresses a week. *A week.* Can you believe it?"

"Kleivenstein, slow down," Alfred pleaded. "I just got in town. Tell me everything about the paper dresses, and start from the beginning."

"It's simple. Scott Paper had this idea of making dresses out of their product. They've already spent millions on advertising, saying the dresses are 'Created to make you the center of conversation at parties, dances and picnics. Wear the dress anytime, anywhere. For kicks, for feeling good, for looking good. Won't last forever? Who cares? It costs almost nothing.'"

"Well, what'd they cost?" Alfred asked.

"The sales price is $1.80 each. The salesman gets sixty cents; I get 30 to cover my expenses."

Avery was waiting. "Kleivenstein, how many salesmen you fixin' to have for this here thing?"

"What do you care?"

"Come on, boy," Avery whined. "You ain't expectin' us to work our tails off with a hundred other salesman on campus, now do you?"

Kleivenstein tilted and started bobbing his head, as if to give him time to think and cushion his response. "Well, I was planning to hire all I could."

"Well, slap my head and call me silly, but I do believe we're wastin' our time here," Avery snapped. "There ain't no deal here."

The rest of us remained silent.

"Look, the media is all over this. They're all saying this phenomenon is here to stay. The throw-away generation is going to love it. It's a big hit in London. You guys are going to make a mint."

Avery stood his ground. "Dadgummit, Kleivenstein, we're your brothers, boy. Here's what we aim to propose. Give the four of us here brothers exclusivity, on campus only, for two weeks. That'll make it right."

It was just enough to bait Kleivenstein. "All right, all right. I'll give you guys two weeks only. Fourteen days, starting this Saturday, and not a day longer. Agreed? I'll bring each of you samples tomorrow, and you can start selling on Saturday."

We all stood and shook his hand. Everyone beamed, except Kleivenstein.

"All right, there it is," Kleivenstein said, and disappeared as quickly as he had appeared.

"I'd like to shake your hand, Avery," Alfred said, extending his hand. "You really came through for us. We are going to make a ton of money."

We all nodded. I was thinking about the nice white wheels and the chrome on the blue '63 Falcon.

"You know, you've got to hand it to Kleivenstein," Mike said. "I don't care what people say about him. The man's fair. He's a good frater."

Avery's eyes flickered. "Kleivenstein agreed too quick. I think the old boy must have a back-up plan or somethin'. Someone like Kleivenstein always has insurance, a Plan B or somethin'."

That evening Kleivenstein had already dropped off a box of samples and order forms. Alfred unsealed the boxes like a five-year old opening a present. The texture was strange, unlike cotton or wool, and the dresses were stiff, like an over-starched shirt.

Alfred placed a sample over himself and wiggled his hips. "It's only a buck eighty," he said. "It'll look good on 'em."

There were no sales strategies or pitch discussions. We'd show up on the lawn by women's dorms, spread out, approach the coeds, and the dresses would sell. What girl wouldn't spend a buck eighty for a dress?

We were wrong. The dresses weren't like hula hoops but more like surfboards in Iowa. Avery and Mike covered the lawn while Alfred and I worked closer to the dorms. We tried everything—coaxing, flattery, lies—some of them were stale: You'll be able to shorten the dresses with scissors; you can scribe notes on them; if it rips, just Scotch tape it; and London's going crazy over these things.

Some of the coeds laughed. "Can I smoke wearing these things?" Or "What if it rains on me?" But most said something to the effect of, "Let me think about it, and I'll see you on the way back to the dorms." There were a few sales but nothing like we'd expected. Avery and Mike did a little better but not much. After a few hours I changed my focus to getting girls' phone numbers, and it surprised me how much easier it was than extracting a buck eighty.

After seven hours of pitching and begging, the four of us re-grouped, ready to call it a day. We sat on the lawn, exhaust-ed. Alfred and I sold 58 dresses between us—a net of $17.40 apiece, about twice minimum wage rate. It wasn't a disaster, but we didn't exactly strike the mother lode.

Mike looked at his sales slips and nodded as if he were moving to music. "Look, this wasn't so bad. We met a lot of coeds, made about twenty bucks apiece, and what else were we going to do anyway?"

"Well, I do declare the sales were slower than a Sunday afternoon, and I'm thinkin' we didn't know what we were doin'," Avery said. "I don't know whether to check my ass or scratch my watch."

The twenty bucks seemed miniscule compared to the $400 I needed. I pictured the Ford in a used car lot, with little pennant flags all over the place and "Special $1500" was painted on the windshield.

Avery was quiet, and I could see his mind was reeling. "Well, butter my butt and call me a biscuit. I got it—I got the answer."

"What? What you talking about?" Alfred asked.

"Look, boys, we only got two weeks. We been sweatin' here like a whore in church on Sunday in a red dress and silver shoes, and we ain't much to show for. At the rate we're goin', this here thing ain't goin' to pay off for us. But, I do believe there's a way."

"Come on, Avery," Mike said, impatient. "What the hell is it?"

"We need to pay no never mind with this one-at-a-time thing on the lawn. What we gotta do is go for quick volume. What we gotta do is get to the fraternities and sororities." He grinned.

There he goes again, I thought. "Why didn't I think of that? The sororities will probably buy more than the frats, right?"

"No, Cort," Avery said. "The fraternities'll buy 'em, invite the sororities to a party, and use 'em as bait."

For the next two weeks, the four of us split up the fraternities and sororities like a marketing region. The social chairmen loved the idea of a paper dress party. There was one problem. They wanted to buy them for the big weekends in November or post-football game bashes well into next month, and there was no cash in the house budget yet. A few of the wealthier houses purchased the dresses immediately, but the profit margin for the two-week work was not much better than the lawn effort. Only a few sororities were interested.

The two-week clause did us in. The four of us pleaded

with Kleivenstein to extend the time limit. Kleivenstein just shook his head and said, "A deal is a deal, guys."

Kleivenstein was going to clean up, and that's in addition to the money the four of us had already handed over. We four fools handed him the fraternity sales on a silver platter. Not only that, Kleivenstein still had all the fraternities and sororities in Syracuse, Rochester, Binghamton, and scores of colleges in the area. The man was going to pocket more from paper dresses than a full professor could make in a year.

I, on the other hand, never got my Falcon, and visions of dates by the lake and weekend ski trips smoldered in flames like burning paper dresses.

SHADES OF GRAY

THE FIRST TIME I met Professor Field, he was hunched over his desk lost in reading, and I learned later that summer he had traveled through some convoluted paths and was not lost at all— even now I think of him at times when faced with doubts or impasses. I had been searching for a summer job after my freshman year when Eric Bell steered me to him. "Just go to Rand Hall, stick your head into Field's office, and ask him if there're any summer positions; it's that simple. He's got money,"

I took Eric's tip.

"Professor Field?" I said meekly.

"Ya, ya, that's me," he said without looking up. "What did I do now? Come on in."

His manner was like his khakis—loose and comfortable. "Sir, my name is Tibor Marston."

"Tibor?" He finally looked up. "Tibor? Are you Hungarian?"

"Er, yes sir. Well, my mother was Hungarian."

"Sit down, son."

He had a trace of European accent, but I couldn't quite place it. Maybe German. "Professor Field, I've come to inquire about a summer job."

"Who told you about a summer job?"

"Eric Bell, your TA. He's a fraternity brother of mine."

"Oh, Eric." The professor chuckled. "Are you intelligent?"

"I guess so, sir."

"You guess so?"

"I mean, I'm all right."

I could tell he liked me, but then maybe he liked everybody. And that's how I got my summer job in 1966—$1.70 an hour as a computer lab assistant, whatever that was. Not only that, there were no set hours. The professor had told me he was a late-nighter and didn't get started 'til ten in the morning. "I'll give you assignments, and you track your hours. There may be days where I'll ask you to work into the evenings, otherwise you're on your own."

This was great, like Tony the Tiger great. Summer in Collegetown. A job. Now all I needed was a place to live. I had hoped to stay at my frat house for the summer, but I'd heard the house was rented to the Scarborough School.

"What's the Scarborough School?" I asked Woody, the house treasurer.

"It's one of those camps but for princesses. About thirty or more of them."

"Princesses?"

"Yeah, JAPs from Long Island. They're too old for camps. So their parents send them up to the Finger Lakes for the summer. The owner of the school arranges for tutors in math and such, then throws in archery, canoeing and shit. Makes a bundle."

"Japs?"

"Jewish American Princess. Jesus, Tibor, you've got some learning to do. Wait a minute; if you're going to be here in the summer, I can arrange a sweet job for you."

"I've already got a job lined up."

"No, it's not a regular job. A waiter, an hour for lunch and an hour for dinner. You get paid, plus all-you-can-eat meals. Oh, and at the end of six weeks you get big tips from the little princesses."

"That sounds good."

"By the way, she usually hires about five waiters, so if you know anybody else..."

"She?"

"Mrs. Simon, the owner of the school," Woody said. "Tibor, you're gonna get laid all summer."

Getting laid all summer? That was some fantasy since I'd never been laid before, though I had let on with the guys that I was no virgin. I'd gotten close before—in high school once and during fall weekend—but no cigar. I think a lot of the other guys were in the same boat. It's not that I was saving myself for love or marriage, though I had long ago left the Catholic Church. Still, I couldn't help thinking of St. Ignatius' words: "Give me the child for seven years, and I will give you the man."

Things were falling into place. Two jobs, no less. Now if I could find a cheap place to live for the summer, well that's all I needed. I didn't actively search for one since as a kid I was told after three good things happen in a row, catastrophe follows. So I became concerned when I immediately found one. I wondered whether superstition followed me, having been an altar boy.

When I mentioned the Scarborough School job to Scotty Newhouse, his eyeballs started to oscillate. "Are you kidding me? Sixteen and seventeen year olds from Long Island? Thirty five of 'em? Damn, I'll wait on them for nothin."

We were check-out clerks at the undergraduate library on Saturday evenings. The library closed after midnight, and Scotty and I had made a habit of sauntering to Collegetown afterwards. We looked like Mutt and Jeff. He was beefy, outgoing and impulsive whereas I was lanky, timid and restrained. He was a theater major; I studied mathematics.

Our only common ground was girls. He had landed a part in *Henry IV* with the Summer Theater, and he told me he was house-sitting his fraternity, Kappa Zeta, alone, for the summer. I could have my choice of the fifteen rooms.

Most students had gone for the summer and the campus was quiet. That morning, the dew vaporized on the grass and the tall elms cast deep shadows against the yellow glow sweeping down the hill. As I ascended Libe Slope from Scotty's frat house, the stillness was broken by the ten o'clock chimes.

Professor Field was already at his office when I walked in. "Tibor, do you know what a modulator demodulator is?" he asked before I even sat down.

"No sir, I don't." First day, first question, and I had no idea what the Professor was talking about. I had taken a couple of programming courses, spending hours at Rand Hall in front of a card machine punching holes onto IBM cards. Five hundred lines of code meant 500 cards of symbols, punched one at a time. I'd submit a stack of cards, and wait hours for printout results. A single error, even a letter or a comma, had to be corrected and resubmitted, then I had to wait hours again. It was like stacking dominoes.

"Let's clear up something, Tibor. You may call me Franz. You are now a colleague and all my colleagues call me Franz."

"I don't know if I can call you that, sir. It wouldn't feel right."

"After the first time, Tibor, it'll be easy." Franz motioned me to follow. "Let me show you our lab where you'll work."

We walked across the hall to an untidy room with a punch-card terminal, scattered IBM cards, printout papers, and a tele-type terminal with a shoebox-size wooden box connected by cables. The box was out of character against all the metal or plastic in the room.

"See this? Franz said, pointing to the box. "This is a modulator demodulator. Some people call it modem. This'll be one of the most important pieces of equipment in the coming years. I am convinced it'll change the world when you are my age."

He flipped the cover, and I saw two circular receptacles the size of a coffee cup. "This is an AT&T modem, 300 baud, with full duplex transmission. It allows computers to transmit data over telephone lines."

"Over telephone lines?"

"I know you're not a computer science major, Tibor, but all this is new technology. In twenty or thirty years every household will have a minicomputer connected to a device like this."

I was skeptical—another professor ranting about how the world was going to change. A computer in every house and hooked up to other computers. I just couldn't picture my mother with an oven-sized machine next to her television.

"You mean someone on a terminal would be able to communicate to a computer across the street? Using telephone lines?"

"Ya, a computer stores information digitally, and as you know information transmitted over a telephone line is transmitted in analog waves," he said, his voiced elevated. "Now, a modem is able to convert between these two forms, and it can send and receive data between two computers. This is an acoustically coupled modem."

Franz dialed a number on the rotary phone. There was garbled hissing, then a high-pitched beep, and then he shoved the phone into the circular receptacles. The teletype terminal started to spit out words. "See, we're connected to Washington. Okay, that's the hardware side. We'll spend more time on the mechanics of its operation later." He waved me over to his office.

This was something out of a science fiction movie. The two computers were talking to each other, like my long distance calls to my mother.

"Now, let me tell you what our little grant is all about. After I come up with modifications to their search engine, you'll connect the terminal with the government computer and run searches, recording the times and search outcomes," Franz said. "Fairly elementary, but these boys in Washington don't know that. We'll have fun this summer."

I was beginning to really like this man.

NO CHANGES WERE needed to the house for the Scarborough School. The open shower area and the urinals in the bathrooms were the only signs the house was meant for men. Mrs. Simon had gathered the five waiters before the first dinner. "Now remember," she said. "These are under-aged girls, and all of you are to remember that. There's to be no cavorting with them."

Woody had told me Mrs. Simon had a good thing going. At fifty, she had lost her husband from a heart attack, leaving her with insurance money and a house. When her two daughters were in high school, she heard all the complaints from the parents about their kids in the summer. "Oy," they had whined. "She sits in front of the tube all day, hogs the phone. They can't work, they can't drive. For three months, kvetch, kvetch, kvetch."

Mrs. Simon remembered that when she decided to go back to work. She spent a little money advertising in the back of *The New York Times* magazine, and she received 34 applications in the first summer, most of them from Long Island, one from North Carolina, and another from Florida. That summer, Mrs. Simon netted $26,500 for eight weeks of work—what a vice president of a small company would earn in a year.

On the first day we stood near the kitchen door as the girls entered the dining room. They marched in jabbering, cigarettes between fingers. Some could pass for thirty, and others had Clearasil covering their zits. Their eyes looked vacant but their mouths cackled like teletype machines.

"Will you look at this?" Scotty said, beaming.

"Scotty, stay away from them. They're trouble." I listened to myself say this, but the words sounded strange, as if I were more mature than he, which I was not.

The other three waiters moved over toward us wearing sheepish grins.

"You see that tall redhead? She's mine," one said. "Boys, this is gonna be a good summer."

The girls began to notice the college men. A couple of them whispered. A few smiled as if they were returning a compliment. They were followed by Mrs. Simon. "Scotty," she called, "go ahead and start serving."

SUMMER IN COLLEGETOWN drew on. I had no set schedule with Franz, and I often read late into the night, windows open to the cooled air and chittering crickets. Some evenings were spent in Sibley Hall's studios where I drew still lifes, charcoal as my medium. I had drawn as long as I could remember—crayons, then pencils, and to acrylic and oils. But charcoal captured me—shading and blending with my fingers or my palm, controlling gradation with varying pressure, turning and rotating to create rich blacks and subtle tonals. Unlike oils, charcoal allowed me to be expressive without spending hours on details, producing art fluently and effortlessly, while mathematics required detailed precision and exactitude.

Summer people huddled in the pubs. I knew the linger-ons and occasionally spent evenings with them into early mornings. They had jobs on campus or were taking classes, but many stayed in town because they had no place to go. They did not want to go home to their families, and they did not want a job or an internship. After only a year of school, Collegetown had become a womb, safe and familiar.

I suppose I was no different. I didn't particularly want go

back to a little suburban town in Ohio to work as a lifeguard or grocery store clerk. My father, a CPA in an insurance company, commuted to Cleveland and had told me I could probably work in the actuarial office; they could always use people to check columns of figures. I thought I'd rather go to a dental office every day.

Near the lake the town dispensed free old-time band concerts, and then there was Summer Theater, cheap movies at the student union, and late afternoon sun-basking on the massive flat shale jutting out of the hillside in the gorge. The Scarborough girls had already fanned out across campus, Collegetown, and even downtown looking for dates.

Scotty had invited a couple of them to the house. First, Phyllis, a short, brown haired, chain-smoking sixteen year old from Valley Stream, then Leslie, a self-avowed socialist with a nose job and burgundy fingernails. Leslie had traveled to Europe the previous year, which made her world-wise. She was against everything: against the war, against suburbs, against two-car garages.

I had warned him more than once but Scotty ignored my cautions. His room was down the hall, but even the closed doors couldn't contain their muffled moans.

"Tibor, these girls are more mature than most of the coeds," he said. "Besides they won't leave me alone."

"They won't leave you alone."

"I'm telling you, she's using me as a guinea pig. She wants me to do things—things I hadn't even thought about."

"What? Like joining the Republican Party?"

"No, no," he laughed. "Every position imaginable. She even wanted to tie me up."

"Give me a break."

"When she's aroused, she claws her fingers into my back. She pants, moans and jabbers lines out of some badly scripted movie."

"Well, you asked for it."

"And she's terrible at faking it. But, that's all right," Scotty said, grinning. "By the way, Tibor, you know that Nina? She keeps asking about you."

"You mean Nina Young? That loner?"

I had noticed Nina in the dining room. Scotty, who made it a point to know all of the girls, had told me Nina grew up in Larchmont. Nina had told him she didn't want to come to the Scarborough School, but her parents insisted that it was either geometry tutorials at the Scarborough School or summer school at Larchmont High. She hated her high school. The idea of getting 250 miles away from her parents convinced her.

Of course I had noticed Nina. She had short curly hair and green catlike eyes, dark circles under them. She had a strong nose and cheek bones. During meals, she stole glances at me. Maybe it was because I wasn't particularly attentive to the girls. It seemed the more aloof I was, the more interesting I became.

"Tibor, she's got the hots for you."

"I'm staying away from her—from all of them," I told him.

"You're such a prude—a Midwestern, uptight, Catholic

prude. Jesus, Tibor, when are you going to grow up?"

Scotty wasn't all wrong. I'd told myself they were all too young, but that wasn't really true. Most of them were only a couple of years younger than I was. As Scotty had pointed out, some were more developed than the coeds. At meals I looked at them, and there were times I became aroused. I did think about some of them when I was alone or when the lights were out. My neocortex held me in check.

The job at the Scarborough wasn't demanding. Add to that Scotty's daily Volkswagen transport service, and it was almost like riding to the other side of the campus for meals. Scotty had set up a routine with Leslie: Leave the school separately and then meet by the suspension bridge at a set time. Driving me back to the house one evening, he said, "Listen, I'll drop you off and then I'm gonna turn around to pick Leslie up."

"Do what you want, Scotty," I said. "Thank God this is the last week of Scarborough. You've been lucky."

"What do you mean by that?"

"I mean you haven't been caught bedding a minor. I mean you haven't knocked her up or anything. I assume."

He laughed. "All the waiters are doing it, except you. And all is well. Besides, I take precautions."

My room was strewn with my sketches of fruits, bowls, trees, portraits, nudes. I went over them at night, making final touches and finishing them with fixatives. I heard Scotty enter the house downstairs and there were other voices.

"Tibor, you here?" Scotty yelled.

Three of them came up the stairs: Scotty, Leslie and Nina. "Surprise," Scotty said, grinning. "You know Nina. She wants to see what a frat house looks like."

"Hi Tibor," Nina said.

Before I could open my mouth, Scotty jumped in. "Listen, would you mind giving Nina a house tour?" With that said, he and Leslie disappeared down the hall into his room, giggling. Scotty caught me off guard; I didn't have time to think whether I was pleased or angry.

Nina read me. "Look, I'm sorry for barging in," she said. "If you want me to, I can walk back to the school."

"No it's okay. Do you really want to see the house?"

"Yeah," she said, her tone changing instantly.

The tour of the house took less than five minutes. When we finally reached my room, her eyes scanned it like sweeping radar, focusing on the charcoals. "Wow, are these all yours?'

"I was just putting my finishing touches."

"These are good," she said, eyes dancing back and forth from one drawing to next. "I didn't know you drew."

"Do you like art?" I asked.

She was holding a handful of my sketches, still examining them. Not looking up, she replied, "Well, I am actually going to be a painter someday. I've been painting all my life."

"Which tutoring class are you taking? Geometry?"

She dropped down on my bed. Looking up at me, she asked, "You mind if I light up?"

"No."

She sucked a big drag, then paused to contain the nicotine, smoke streaming from her puckered mouth. For the moment, she seemed mature. She looked at me and spoke deliberately. "I'm supposed to have a 150 IQ, but I hate school. I hate math. I hate history. I hate chemistry. I hate everything but art."

"Are you planning to go to college?" I asked.

"Hell no. I might go to art school—maybe out on the West Coast. As far from Larchmont as possible."

"Your parents may not be happy about that, Nina."

"My parents aren't going to be happy about lots of things. I'm not going to live near home. I am not going to college. I'm not going to get a steady job. I'm not going to get married. And, I'm not going to have babies."

"So what are you going to do?" I asked.

"I'm going to paint. I'm going to have lovers, lots of lovers. And I'll trade in my lovers like cars—about every three years." She tapped her butt into a Styrofoam cup. "Do you have any wine?"

"You're not old enough." I was patronizing her and knew I sounded awkward.

"I'll be seventeen in November. In China, a baby is considered a year old at birth. That makes me eighteen in a few months."

"You're not Chinese. I'll go to jail for corrupting a minor."

"You're only a couple of years older than me. President Kennedy was twelve years older than Jackie."

Nina's green eyes, as Scotty had pointed out, reminded me

of a cat. She wasn't intimidated by anyone, least of all me, and I gave in. I went downstairs to the kitchen and grabbed the opened bottle of Chablis. When I entered my room, she had turned off all the lights but the desk lamp, and she was fully undressed. She ambushed me from the back, surrounding my waist with her arms, her breasts firmly against me. She kissed my neck.

"Hold on, Nina," I said.

"We haven't got time. I'll be going back to Larchmont in a week."

Her breasts were perfect, her hips round. I was fully aroused, and I wanted to grab her. But when I was in third grade, Sister Catherine had read stories to us after lunch, mostly from the Bible or stories with moral punches. One of the sister's stories that I remember, and which emerges irregularly, had the devil whispering in one ear of a man and an angel in the other. Maybe St. Ignatius was right after all.

"Nina, I like you," I said, not believing my own ears. "But I think you better put your clothes on."

Nina didn't protest. She paused to look at me and kissed me, and then she began to dress. I watched her pick up her bra and snap the hooks from the front side beneath her breasts; she then turned her bra around her torso. I'm not sure why, but I was stirred again and was having serious second thoughts. But it was too late. Also, I didn't think Nina was that disappointed, possibly even relieved. Rather than waiting for Scotty, I walked her back.

Tension was high on Friday, the day before the chartered

buses and parents were to return the girls home. The girls had pledged themselves to lose their virginity or fall in love over the summer. They wanted to make the most of the last evening, their last opportunity. Nina didn't say much at dinner, and she avoided eye contact as she had done all week. Like most girls in the dining room, Scotty and the other waiters had already made plans for the evening and were anxious to finish their chores. When we were busing the tables, the girls thanked us with little kisses on cheeks and envelopes stuffed with five and ten dollar bills.

I told Scotty I had some work at Rand Hall and left Scarborough early. I walked slowly, annoyed at the stuffy evening air and wished I had just waited for Scotty's ride. The office wasn't any better. There was a floor fan in one corner of the room, but the heavy air didn't move much. Franz was on the punch-card machine, pecking with his index fingers. Sweat beaded on his forehead.

He looked up. "Tibor, I didn't know you were coming by. I'm glad you're here; I could use a break and some company."

"I just finished my last day at the Scarborough School, and I needed some of the earlier printouts for my weekly report."

"Ah, the Scarborough School. All those young high school girls. And did you have a good summer with them?"

He wanted to talk and took his glasses off to clean them, using a corner of his plaid shirt. We hadn't socialized much before, and I didn't know much about him—whether he was married, children, or where he lived. And there hadn't been anyone on campus who could tell me. But he seemed amused about the young girls.

"Well sir, they're quite young, and ..."

Franz laughed. Then he laughed some more. "You're young too, Tibor."

"Sir, they're below age. And I...the others didn't let anything stop them. But, I was more concerned."

His laughter slowed, but a grin remained on his face. Franz's ebullience surprised me, and at the same time I became more comfortable with him. I said, "Maybe I shouldn't be so straight. So straight-arrow. I don't know. I should be more like my roommate."

"Young people will do what they have to do. Just don't hurt anyone along the way." The grin disappeared, as if he was thinking of something far away.

"Have you ever been married?" I blurted.

Now Franz was surprised. He turned to face me, placing his left hand on his cheek. "I was in love once, in college, but it was illegal for us to marry." His eyes moved to another direction, and his face was emotionless. The drone of the fan and harsh fluorescent lights added to the silence.

I was puzzled. Did he mean that she was underage? Was his love a foreigner or an illegal? Was he gay? Were they related? I didn't have the courage to ask him, but while I was thinking these questions, something hit me. Franz had rolled up his long sleeve shirt to his elbows, and on the inner side of his left upper forearm were a handful of bluish numbers, tattooed digits. I had seen these before in Movietone newsreels at the movies—Allied armies liberating Jews in concentration camps and little children extending their arms for the cameras. My throat grew parched, and I coughed to regain my composure. I excused myself and I sensed he understood what I had noticed.

The streetlights had turned on when I walked out of the building, and the dusk added to my aloneness. Standing atop Libe Slope, I focused on the faint lights in the valley. I raised my head toward West Hill and made out just a shaded outline, the faltering glow about to be snuffed out. I didn't want to think about Franz. Instead I thought a charcoal, or a painting, could never quite capture the nuances of light and shadow.

Scotty's Beetle was parked by the front door of his frat. As I went inside, I thought about how he and Leslie didn't have much time left. I moved beyond the large living room to the refrigerator in the kitchen and picked up a 7-Up. Heading up the stairs, I heard the familiar thumping and groaning from Scotty's room.

The lights in my room were off, and I opted to use only the desk light and turned the radio volume low, shrouding unwanted sounds from the hallway. Thoughts of what I had seen at the office remained, and I immersed myself in my charcoals, staring blankly at them. I had forgotten about Scotty and Leslie, their noise having ceased a while before, but the silence was broken by a door latch. I thought about remaining in front of my desk. After all, I really didn't know Leslie very well. But, I changed my mind, my legs needing some stretching. I thought I might as well say my polite good bye to her.

When I left my room, they were already in the hallway. The girl wasn't Leslie, but Nina. I stood still. She walked towards me, looked at me, started to move her mouth, but tured away and descended the stairs. Scotty followed her and said casually, "Tibor, I'm going to take her to the house. Back in a bit."

I wasn't sure I was hurt, but I was upset. Nina was not my girl and we didn't even know each other. And we certainly hadn't been intimate. Was I jealous of Scotty? That didn't make sense. Angry with him? That didn't make sense either. Scotty didn't show guilt or shame.

I considered waiting for Scotty to confront him, but there was really nothing to say. Tired, I sat on my bed and took off my brown loafers, Professor Field's words resurfacing: "Just don't hurt anyone along the way."

EDGE CITY

HAD I NOT run into Mara Shipley when I returned to school in September, I would never have fallen in love with Jenny, and I would have wound up in Vietnam—I'm quite certain. Two years earlier I'd been back home in Portland, Maine, having taken a leave from my studies after completing my junior year; nobody did that but I'd had it with school. I was burned out, losing interest in my studies, and I had failed in a year-long relationship. After I completed my last exam that spring, I packed my suitcase, my stereo, and a few books, pointed my Ford Pony towards Route 13 and left town.

"Garr? Garr Boothe?" Someone tapped my shoulder.

I took a second to recognize Mara, her anemic coloring and lifeless hair conveying glumness absent when she was dating my friend, Skip O'Toole.

"Mara. Let's see, you're a senior now, right? I heard Skip was off to grad school in Chicago. I thought you'd be with him."

"Right. He split right after he got his degree."

Split? When had she started using words like that? "Too bad."

"How about you, Garr, what's happenin' with you?"

"Well, you know I been living back home for the last couple of years, and I came back to finish. But idiot me, I hadn't thought much about where I'd live. I'm looking for a place now, as we speak."

"Try La Casa."

"What's that?"

"Like, it's a group house down off Buffalo Street, a huge Victorian with lots of rooms. And the people are solid. Ask for a chick named Ali Garske—she's good people."

Good people?

We said our goodbyes but then she turned. "Wait Garr, do you remember Randy Warwick? I think he was in your class."

"Yeah, I remember him." He and Skip had hung out but we weren't close.

"He graduated last year but he's still living in town. He's up on Dryden, 505 Dryden, and I think he may be searching for someone to live with."

I didn't think I'd want to room with this guy Randy, but I wasn't sure why. Maybe I didn't like the jacket and tie he'd worn to class or the way he parted his hair. Besides, La Casa was right around the corner and I had never been in a group house, probably full of coeds.

As I walked through Collegetown, I was suffused with the smell of maple leaves and goldenrod, and I looked to a new start with familiar feelings. Meanwhile the country was starting to go crazy. The war in Vietnam was escalating, Martin Luther King and Robert Kennedy had been assassinated, race riots were breaking out in hot cities across the country. In August Chicago police had beaten hundreds of marchers at the Democratic convention. America was shifting. Kids talked of flower power, love-ins and drugs. The music was changing as well, from the Beach Boys and bubble gum music to new-starts like Jimmy Hendrix and Janis Joplin. But along with the rumblings, campus life hummed along at an accustomed pace—football games, homecoming and lawn parties.

My previous classmates had already graduated, so coming back felt like being a freshman again. Eddy Street was noisy with backed up traffic, people talking on street corners, and rock music blasting from apartment windows. Longer hair, bandanas, bell-bottoms, and tie-dyed shirts had infiltrated the standard style though the majority of students still appeared and dressed not different from the 1950s.

La Casa had been used as a small hospital in the previous century. The front struck me as if it had been modeled after an Edger Allan Poe story: dark gray paint, gables and square windows. The door was left half open and when I walked into the dimmed foyer, a smell of incense hit me like musty hay in an abandoned barn. Voices came from the back rooms, but Bob Dylan on the stereo made hearing what they were saying difficult. Candles flittered on every surface in the living room. What had Mara been thinking?

"Hello, is anyone here?" I yelled. "Hello? Is Ali Garske around?"

A couple, one of them holding a spatula, poked their heads from the back room, the kitchen I presumed, and slipped back. Already I had made up my mind and turned to leave.

"I'm Ali. Can I help you?"

She wasn't what I'd expected. Except for her faded jeans, she was not unlike other coeds—no makeup, short brown hair, a pleasant smile. Her hands were slightly wet.

"I'm a friend of Mara Shipley, and she told me there might be a room available here."

"Come sit," she said and led me to the living room. Three dirty sofas, a couple of stained chairs, and mismatched table lamps decorated what may have once been an elegant room. "I'm sorry but the house is full right now. There's a chance someone might not show up for the semester, but even that may not help. We've quite a waiting list."

A couple came in the front door talking and scurried up

the stairs. The red-headed scrawny guy had a scraggly beard and mustache like a Chinese sage, his long hair needing a wash. The coed could have been his sister, skinny with a headband that resembled a decorative ribbon from a sewing box.

"This place isn't affiliated with the school, is it?"

She laughed. "No, no," she said, still laughing. "It's a co-op. We all share work. Cooking, cleaning, buying food. There're no officers like the fraternities but we have Initiators. It's only our second year, but we're tight."

A worker's paradise with Initiators, whatever they are. I stood up. "Well, I'm sorry there's no space. Thanks for your time. You've been kind." Maybe I'd have to live downtown. Away from campus, I'd have to deal with parking.

I DIDN'T RECOGNIZE Randy when I walked into his place on Dryden. His mustache hung down to his chin. His wire rims, bangs, and moppy haircut made him resemble John Lennon. He appeared younger than the days when he had worn his button-down Oxfords and manicured hair.

"Hey Garr," he said in a loud pitch. "Man, I haven't seen you in ages. I'd heard you took a leave."

I recalled him having cautious mannerisms, but now he seemed open and at ease. "Yeah, I was back home. Had a job working as a draftsman in a little engineering company. I'm going to finish out the degree this year."

The house was a two-story, each floor remodeled as a separate rental unit. Randy's apartment had three bedrooms:

two large ones and a closet-sized cubbyhole barely big enough for a bed and a desk, where someone had painted "Edge City" on the door. Randy told me the two larger rooms were taken, the largest for himself and the other by a Jeff Southward and his girlfriend Kathy Brownly, who had her own place in Collegetown, but she'd already moved her clothes and books into Jeff's room. "Her parents might be coming up to see her," Randy explained. "She wanted to hold on to her own place in case she needs to show them where she lived."

Randy was glad to see me though I wasn't sure why. "Garr, if you want Edge City, you can have it, man. Kathy had said she'd pay her share of the rent, so we hadn't thought about renting it out. But if you're stuck, it's yours. Besides it'll lower everyone's rent."

"Don't you have to get your roommates to agree on this?"

"Not really, it's my lease. They'll be fine with you, I'm sure of it. Jeff's good people and you'll like Kathy. They went down to get some food and should be back soon."

When Jeff and Kathy walked in, they had fixed smiles as if they knew a secret. Jeff stomped in in his Frye boots, shiny and neatly polished. He wore bellbottoms over his long skinny legs, a wide-collared chartreuse shirt, and a clean headband with a stripped end dangling over his left ear like a single feather on a Cheyenne scout. A silver clip held Kathy's long brown hair back, a Bloomingdale purse over her shoulders. She wore a peasant blouse embroidered with tiny red flowers. She was pretty and he was handsome. They both welcomed me into the house as if I were a lost puppy dog.

"Solid. Oh, this is far out, man," Jeff said, after Randy told them they had a new apartment mate.

Randy had been Jeff's big brother at Delta Beta house, but both left the frat life for Collegetown. They weren't really rebels or hippies, but they agreed with the idea of being rebels, of 'veering away from the system' as they called it. When Jeff and Kathy walked together on campus, people turned their heads—people like me.

Kathy had been a sister at the Gamma Xi house on Thurston Avenue and popular in the fraternity circles. The Gamma girls were known to be the sweet and pretty ones, unlike the Omega girls who were rich and bitchy, or the Delta girls who were supposed to be wholesome. It was Kathy who gave me the lead to my job. "The Gamma house is always short of dishwashers. I think their pay is okay and you get all meals free. I can call Jenny at the house and set you up if you'd like."

Even living at home, I was amazed how little I'd saved the past two years. My father made a comfortable living. Still, sending a kid through college was a bit of stretch for him, and even with my savings from my drafting job, I was little short. Free meals and pocket money would help. Most good jobs like library work were long gone. So I took Kathy's advice and walked across campus to her old sorority.

"DINNER FOR THE staff is served promptly at 5:30 during the week days," Jenny said. "Once the house dinner is served, you'll start with the pots and pans, then move onto the plates and silverware. The pay is $2.10 per hour." She tried to be business-like, but she couldn't pull it off. Her voice was too soft, and her large glossy-chocolate eyes overly trusting. I soon learned Jennifer Radford was the house business manager, which meant she took care of the bills, house repairs and meals.

I liked studying her while she rattled off business points. Her eyebrows were thin and symmetrical, and her nose was narrow, slightly turned up. She had a habit of moving her shoulder-length brown hair to hide her small ears, and her lips stretched wide when she smiled.

Crisp temperatures and relentless clouds hovered over campus through much of the fall, the last of the wizened leaves clinging onto elm trees against Canadian winds. My classes moved smoothly, seeming more informal and less intense than in past years; whenever I had flashbacks of Portland, working all day and tired at night, I was pleased to be a student again.

All of us at the apartment ate together on weekends. I only saw Jeff and Kathy on and off during the week, but Randy usually could be found at the apartment working on his car. He had a '47 Daimler in the house garage that he'd been fixing for years. I once saw him stay up all night rebuilding the carburetor. Hundreds of little parts—nuts, bolts, screws, springs—were placed in separate dishes filled with alcohol, strewn on the floor of his room like Monet's water lilies.

Randy was originally in my class and had graduated the

year before, but he told me he decided to just hang out in town rather than going to grad school or getting a job. He'd spend part of his days at the student union, sitting hours on end in a chess game or in some bullshit session. Or he'd be in the reference section of the graduate library reading a half a dozen newspapers.

He was part of the Boston Brahmin, the oldest established families in America. There were about twenty of them in all, and they acquired their wealth not exactly in a noble way, he had told me. In the eighteenth century it was the triangle trade with Africa for slaves and rum; smuggling and gun running during the Revolutionary War; delivering opium to the Chinese when British ships were prohibited from entering the Chinese ports in early 1800s; later moving to textiles and chemicals, and finally to banking in the twentieth. Not only that, for the past two centuries, they'd been consolidating their wealth by marrying each other.

THE FALL SEMESTER hurried through, presidential campaign issues dominating campus discussions: race riots, the counterculture movement, New Left movement, Black Power movement, and of course, the war.

On the last day of October, a Canadian high pressure system brought in white, desert-like sunlight as if it was reparation for a two-week continuum of clouds, cold rain, and more clouds. At noon the bell tower chimed "You are My Sunshine," and though it was still nipping cold, everyone pranced on the Arts Quad lawn as if they were little kids let out from school. Near the undergraduate library, I spotted a hand waving in the air, motioning to me. Jenny had a red beret and a long scarf wrapped around her neck, her cheeks aflush from the cold. "Garr!" she yelled.

Her classes were finished for the day, and she was on her way back to the house when I asked her to have lunch at the student union. She was quick to accept.

"You old enough to vote, Jenny?" I asked sitting down with a tray of lunch.

"I turned 21 this past summer but I'm not sure who I'll vote for. Humphrey'll just continue Johnson's policies which are really no different than Nixon's, or Wallace's for that matter. I might just write in McCarthy. How about you?"

"My first presidential election. But I don't think I'll vote at all—I can't stand any of them."

"My father's pushing me towards Humphrey," she said. "He's probably one of six people who's voting Democrat in Darien."

I knew Darien was one of the oldest and wealthiest towns in America, but I said nothing.

"He's a high school history teacher there, not your typical Darien resident."

"I see. Which explains your scholarship and your job at Gamma."

"Yep. What about you, Garr? What are your plans after graduation?"

"Not sure. The draft is looming over me, but even without that, I'm not sure."

"Not even grad school?" There was a tone of angst in her voice.

"I really don't know, Jenny."

Even serious, her doe-eyes exuded warmth. She told me that when she was twelve, she had contracted a rare spine ailment, and for two years she was restricted to bed and in grueling pain. Therapy was even more unbearable. Mostly she read history during her confinement, and she had memorized every English monarch from William the Conqueror to Elizabeth II. She did well in high school, taking all the advanced courses and singing lead in the choir. She was on a university scholarship, probably the only sister in the house whose father wasn't paying her tuition.

Though she readily talked about herself, she also asked about me and my home and snuck in questions about my family economics.

WE WERE WELL into the second semester. Tuesdays were my longest days. When I crossed the bridge over the gorge separating the campus from the coed dorms, I couldn't even tell whether the sun had set. The opaque clouds hid the valley below the campus, and the West Hill was a continuous blur.

The sorority house parking lot was full, the snow flattened by fresh tire tracks. Upper-class sisters often showed up for dinner, and that meant we washed as many as 40 place settings of dishes, plates, bowls and glasses, plus forks, spoons and knives. I figured Gorvoy, the other dishwasher, and I had washed over 20,000 dishes and plates along with 14,000 pieces of silverware over the past six months.

Stanley Gorvoy had kinky red hair, thousands of freckles, and was 40 pounds overweight. When he laughed, the fat surrounding his eyes crinkled up and made him look like a sumo wrestler. He was the captain of the debate team and on his way to Yale Law. He drove around the campus on a Vespa scooter bike, which looked as if it was about to collapse under him.

Earlier in the year, Gorvoy had noticed I was washing each glass with a brush. "Whoa. Hold on there," he said. "It'll take you four times as long the way you're washing those glasses. Fill up this tub with hot water, dump in a little detergent, and then just dunk the glass. Put the glass in the draining tray. Afterwards just spray the glasses with water. That's it. There's no need for scrubbing. There's no food stuck to these glasses. Washing glasses with a brush is bullshit. Don't let Jenny see you though."

I started to notice the change in Jenny after the term break. At first she had only eaten with the kitchen help when she had a paper deadline or an exam, and then cut out to the library before the house dinner. But she began to eat with us more, making excuses for it. Right after the spring recess, I was washing dishes, plunging my hands into the soapy water, a fixed sour look on my face, and I caught her looking at me. At first I thought she was feeling sorry for me— sometimes I felt sorry for myself—but it dawned on me that she wasn't. When she ate with us, she avoided making eye contact with me. I'd lock on her, but she wouldn't look my way. Which convinced me she had a crush on me.

I'd been in love once, a couple years before. Her name was Laura Burke, and she'd lived with three other coeds in a house on Delaware Avenue across the street from where I rented a little studio. I'd catch her walking to class early mornings and we became intimate very quickly. By Thanksgiving of that fall, she'd already moved in, and by Easter of the following spring she wanted to marry me. I loved her, but she scared me when she behaved as if she had a deadline to meet. I'd read too many novels and seen too many movies where a young marriage quickly falls apart after a few years. Before the semester ended, she had moved out and found another lover. Seeing her with another guy hurt, and I wondered if I had made a dreadful mistake.

Over the past couple of years, I realized I didn't know anything about love. I had been happy with Laura. Living with her, eating with her, sleeping with her, and just being with her. So, why couldn't I commit? I'd never had much trouble finding girls. In high school, girls would say I resembled Richard Breymer, the lead actor in *West Side Story*. I didn't think I looked like him.

When Jenny started to send signals she was interested, I didn't encourage her at first. Maybe the burn from Laura was still there. But also I had never paid much attention to the sorority girls; they were too into themselves, and the Gamma girls were no different. But the more I tried not to think about Jenny, the more she stayed on my mind. As my engineering professor talked of vector forces, I found myself doodling her name in my notebook.

One evening Gorvoy was going on in front of the waitresses about all the coming political changes with a new president in Washington. Jenny didn't eat with us. I didn't say much or eat my usual second serving. I watched for Jenny.

The sisters were finishing their dinners, and Gorvoy and I were done with the pots and pans. Before we got to the dinner plates, we usually took a smoke break in the pantry.

"You're stuck on her, aren't you, you schnook?" he said.

"What are you talking about?"

"You know who I'm talking about. Jenny. Look Garr, I'm going to give you some unsolicited advice, something I don't usually do, but I like you. Forget her."

I stared at him.

"You know she's getting married to some rich putz. It's over. She likes you, Garr, but she's just not going to just pass up zillions of dollars."

"She is? Who is he?"

"Oy. You're such a schmuck. All these broads in this house are the same. I guarantee you Jenny's no different. She's a little better than the others, but she's no different."

"What's his name?"

"I've heard his name mentioned. Bill Kirk, I think. Some fraternity guy."

Why hadn't Jenny mentioned him all this time? Not that she needed to, but thinking about it, I wondered if she'd gone out of her way to hide it. I'd never even seen her with a guy.

I was bothered by what Gorvoy said, probably because he was always right. He had known Jenny for several years and knew a few things about her. Her father did teach in high school, and they did live in a modest house near the town center surrounded by Georgian and Tudor mansions. Jenny had told Gorvoy that her parents had fought over money, eventually divorcing over it.

For the most part I spent my weekends in the apartment. The kitchen was closed at the Gamma house on weekends. Saturdays, the sisters went on dates, and Sundays were open to their whims. At the apartment Jeff and Kathy made dinner, or Randy, who was a gourmet cook, while I was left to do the dishes. Other than at meals Jeff and Kathy were usually locked in their room, but I spent time with Randy when I wasn't booking.

I was putting the dishes away after dinner and Randy was reading his *Times*. "This is heavy, Garr. Have you heard the latest on the draft? Graduate students won't be able to maintain their deferment status anymore."

"Are you kidding me?"

"That's what the paper says."

I stopped washing the dishes and grabbed his paper. "Let me see this."

At the time students were guaranteed a II-S, or student deferment. As a matter of fact, I would have stayed home another year had my draft board not asked me questions about my status at school. When I got my second letter asking me to confirm my enrollment, I grew nervous. "Damn,

now what am I going to do? I'm not keen on basic training—
I've heard horror stories—let alone carrying a damn rifle in
the jungle."

Randy knew the options already. "Well, you could split to
Canada, or you could claim to be a conscientious objector, or
join the National Guard, or get some kind of a medical
deferment. There are also deferment jobs with defense
companies like Grumman Aircraft on Long Island, but then
you'd be designing war machines. Or you could do what Jeff's
planning to do."

"What the hell's that?"

"Get married. And even better, have kids—you'll double
your insurance. Getting married isn't a guarantee but it's
pretty safe. Otherwise you're 1-A, ready for Uncle Sam's fuckin' army.

"What's your status? You're obviously not II-S."

"Nope, not for about a year. I even had to go down to
Richmond for a physical."

"Why Richmond?"

"Because my parent's address, and mine, is officially in
Virginia. My father's in the Foreign Service in Washington
but lives in Alexandria."

"So what is your status?"

"1-A. But it's under appeal," he said calmly.

"Appeal?"

"Well, my father knows a shrink in Boston and he wrote a
letter stating I was a homosexual."

"What?"

"It's true. Not about me being a homosexual, but our shrink friend who wrote the letter is very anti-war and was glad to do it. Draft boards consider homosexuality a deviance. It gets you a 4-F—unqualified for military duty."

"Jesus, Randy. That's going to follow you all your life—officially documented that you're gay."

"I really don't give a shit."

I could see that. Randy had money; he wasn't planning to get into politics, and he had no interest in the corporate life. He and everyone else knew he was straight. So what if the United States government thought he was gay?

"Did you really have a physical already? What was that like?"

Randy chuckled and grabbed his coffee mug. "I get this letter from my Selective Service telling me I had to get on this bus in Arlington for Richmond at six in the morning; can you believe that? Six AM. Let's see, that was June 9th last year. The day after my birthday. I pulled an all-nighter, thinking that might help me flunk the physical. Anyway I get on the bus, jam-packed, and there must have been about 80 of us. I sit next to this kid and he says, 'God, I hope I can pass the test.' I had been thinking of all kinds of ways to flunk, but it shook me to think not everyone felt the way I did. In Richmond the whole busload streamed into this building—I think it was part of the National Guard Armory—and in the reception room, a real uptight sergeant welcomes us, 'Everyone take the papers the private is handing out. Fill out the form on the first page only, then strip down and move into the room down the hall. Go to the door with the letter of your last name. If you have trouble filling out the form, look at the poster.' And he points to a large cardboard paper with a filled-out form. You won't believe this, Garr, but the sample name that was on the form was Peter Small—I swear it's true."

"Unbelievable," I said waiting for him to go on.

Randy sipped his coffee slowly as if to pause like an actor crafting his timing. He liked telling this story.

"Well, I filled out the form," he continued. "Some guys were spending fifteen minutes to finish the simple form; I don't think it even took up a page. Then I went to the room down the hall. There were guys, buck naked with their clothes on the floor, standing next to a wall. Some had their hands cupped over their wazoos. They clearly weren't digging the situation. Anyway I too stripped and remained in anticipation. Eventually about a dozen of us filled the room, all naked, all silent, and all peeking. We waited in suspense, waited until a balding man in a white coat came into the room, shut the door, and introduced himself as Dr. Bernard. He had a fixed grin and was skinny—couldn't have been more than five-four. He gives us this shrill command, 'Now boys, you will stand to form a big circle around me, and then you will do as I instruct like the Simon Says game. Understand?' Then he lifted his chin to start the game.

"So," I said, "you've got this little man surrounded by a dozen boys, stripped naked with their dongs hanging down, with stupid looks on their faces. Unbelievable."

Randy let out a forced laugh. "Yup. The little man started to give orders. 'Boys, I want you to stretch out your arms and rotate them; you'll have to move further out to form a bigger circle first.' We started to rotate our arms, and I couldn't help thinking we were staging a naked ballet for this Tinker Bell in the middle of the ring. Then the doctor proceeded to give these ridiculous commands: touch your nose with your pinky, stand on one leg, raise your arms, twirl your arms, and such; it was so fuckin' unreal. Then he went around the circle and examined each one of us—our eyes, throat, reflex, and of course our little gonads. The final instruction from him was the best. 'Now boys, do an about face and bend as if you're gonna touch your toes.' Can you picture it? With twelve boys in a circle with their butts in the air, he proceeded to give us a rectal, one by one. The man put on a rubber glove and poked a dozen assholes, each guy screaming ooh's and aah's."

I was laughing hard and had trouble stopping. "So I guess you passed the physical," I finally said.

"The final phase of the physical was the intelligence test, sort of a watered-down version of an IQ test—pretty simple, really. Believe it or not, I even tried to flunk it. I figured they weren't going to believe an engineering grad was dumb enough to flunk their test. So I took a shot and tried to put myself just below passing, like a point below the passing score. Even then I evidently passed it. Several weeks later I got my I-A, and that's when I called our family friend, the shrink."

Jeff and Kathy came out of their room holding hands. Kathy had a beatific smile on her face. I thought, how do you hold hands after spending all that time together?

"What is happening?" Jeff asked.

"I was just telling Garr about my physical."

"That's funny shit."

"You heard about them getting rid of deferment for graduate school?" I asked.

"Yeah. The marriage deferment is still good though, right?" Jeff asked.

"As far as anyone knows," Randy said. "But who the hell knows what'll change in the future. When you get tied, better have some kids, quick."

Kathy giggled. "I'm for that."

"You guys wanna get stoned? I just got a dime bag from Blackie. It's good shit."

Blackie was Jeff's supplier, and like Randy, he'd hung around town after graduating. I'd heard Blackie had a connection, and he'd disappear to the city for a few days every other month. He looked like a freak and always traveled in the middle of the night, figuring he had less chance of getting stopped by a cop. Get busted with dope and you were in serious trouble in New York state. I'd heard stories of people getting six to ten for just possession.

Randy often joined them to get high in the evenings, though Jeff and Kathy usually held off until the weekend. I had resisted grass all this time, something in my puritan New England background, I supposed. Besides I couldn't afford it.

But that night, with news of the new draft rules, I wanted to see what all this dope stuff was about.

"Screw it," I said. "Let's get high."

"Dig it!" Jeff said. "Kathy, can you get candles and the dope from the room, and let's turn out the florescent."

So we sat around the kitchen table, lights out and candles lit. Jeff put on his new Stones' *Sympathy for the Devil* album.

I watched Jeff remove a square piece of cigarette paper from a matchbox-sized box. Then with a coffee stirrer he'd saved from McDonalds, he carefully separated the dried leaves he'd placed on a typing paper and moved them to his roll-paper. He resembled a lab technician. Jeff pressed his lips tight as he started to fold the joint, licked the paper, and gave the ends of the stick a little twist. "Give me a match," he said, then lit the joint.

While I was studying his movements in the candlelight, I couldn't help wondering what had drawn him to the counterculture. Could it have been the drugs and music, or political issues like the war and race problems? Or was it fashion or personal? He was from Lake Forest near Chicago, and his father was a successful investment banker. At dinner earlier in the fall, Jeff had told us how his father would often have different meals than the rest of the family. "The bastard would have Porterhouse steak while the rest of us ate ground chuck." Jeff was angry.

Jeff inhaled deeply and closed his eyes, his shoulders raised. It was a good five seconds before he slowly released the smoke. "This is good shit. Wow, man, this is good shit."

His eyes were still closed. He passed the joint to Kathy, who carried on a similar ceremony.

"Here, Garr," she said to me. "Take it in deep."

I sucked hard, held it a while, and let loose. "I don't feel a thing," I said.

They all laughed. "Wait," Randy said. "It'll come."

I sat back in my chair and stared at the ceiling while I waited for my hit to come around. Kathy was already giggly and looked at me as if I should giggle as well. Jeff had his arms around her, stroking her upper arms, and nodding his head up and down like some Buddhist in a chant. And Randy was digging the Stones.

"I'm in love," I blurted, still staring at the ceiling.

All heads turned to me. "Are you kidding? Who?" Randy asked.

"Her name is Jenny Radford."

"Jenny?" Kathy asked, sobering. "Jenny at the house? She's engaged, Garr. Got engaged last spring."

"To William Kirk," I said.

"Jesus, Garr," Randy said. "Jeff and I know Bill. He was in our old fraternity, and he was in our class. Government major, I think. "

I sat up. "Yeah? Is he still in town?"

"No," Randy said. "He left for Stanford Law last year."

"He is one uptight dude," Jeff said. "But he's old money, man. Rich, from San Francisco."

Kathy let out a long drag. "Couple of years ago, Jenny had this crush on Frank Harvey, and then she found out he was gay, and as it turned out, it was Frank who introduced Jenny to Bill, who was Frank's roommate at the time."

"Wow, I think you're stoned, Kath," Randy said, blinking.

"That's some heavy shit," I said.

Everyone laughed, even me. What am I doing talking like Jeff now, I asked myself. The euphoria was getting to me. And soon everything was funny.

I was living in two worlds. Here I was getting high and surrounded by people who spoke a different language and dressed like gypsies. The sorority sisters wore pearl necklaces and spoke like women fifty years earlier. I wondered where I belonged.

THE DAY BEFORE spring break, I had finished the pots and pans at the sorority. Jenny had continued her guarded behavior, and it was beginning to annoy me. I'd been searching for an opening with her, but it was as if she sensed that. I said goodnight to everyone in the kitchen after I dried the last pan and walked out the back door. That's when I saw her in the parking lot.

"Jenny, where are you going?" I shouted and ran to her.

"Library."

"Jesus, everyone else is getting ready to leave town," I said.

"I've got some catching up to do on a couple of courses."

"If you're going to bury yourself in the carrels, I'll go with you. I've got work too."

She surprised me. "If you'd like."

Snow powdered the sidewalks, and flakes swirled around against the amber streetlights— a noiseless evening. Jenny walked next to me, glancing over occasionally, and I tried to slow my heartbeat. When she almost lost her balance on a patch of snow, she wrapped her arm around mine and kept it there. We didn't speak much.

Half of the students had already left town, and the stacks were empty and dead quiet. Jenny found her usual carrel on the third floor and I sat behind her, a wide stack separating us. Other than a bespectacled redhead, we had the floor to ourselves. There were moments I was tempted to get up to see Jenny, but I didn't.

After three hours she stood up and walked over. "Garr, I think I've had it."

"You feel like some food, or a drink?"

"I don't know. It's getting late, don't you think?"

It was her "Don't you think" that did it. "Come on," I said. "It's only 10:30."

I thought about asking her to my apartment. After all, she already knew Kathy. On the other hand, that might make her refuse.

Outside the blistery wind had picked up. I grabbed her book bag and wrapped my arm around her shoulders. She didn't resist. It was only a ten-minute walk to the Palms Bar in Collegetown, and it went by too fast.

Unlike the stacks the bar was crowded, thick with smoke and noise. Before sitting down Jenny looked around as if she was about to steal a candy. When she got her cheeseburger and her gin and tonic, she took a big gulp.

"Mm, that's good," she said putting down her drink to grab her burger.

I'd been studying her face all these months, and I still liked looking at the dimple she had on only one side. Her lips half-puckered occasionally.

"Jenny, I've been wanting to be with you for months now," I said.

"Please, Garr, you know I'm engaged."

"Yeah, I heard, you really gonna marry this guy?"

She faced down and shook her drink. "Of course I'm going to marry Bill, right after graduation. My parents think he's wonderful and so do all my sisters."

"Your parents?"

"Bill flew all the way from San Francisco to meet them last summer to ask for my hand. He's very thoughtful."

Thoughtful? Captain Kangaroo is thoughtful, I said to myself, but you don't have to marry him.

Jenny didn't look at me and I was sure she knew she sounded defensive. She continued to drink her gin, and after a second one she breathed a deep sigh. "Garr? Garr, I want to say something to you," she said, her eyes swimming. "I think about you often. I think about you all the time. I think about you at night." Her voice cracked.

I reached out to her.

She said, "Garr, please take me back to the house."

The walk back to Gamma was long. We hardly said a word. On the one hand I was happy she made her confession.

On the other, where did it get me? She was set on marrying this guy, period. The street lights lit the bridge near her house, but it was empty, the sidewalks now piling up with more snow. The drinks had gotten to her. When I grabbed her elbow to steady her, she said, "Thanks, Garr," and looked up.

I dropped the books and kissed her; she wrapped her arms around my neck tightening our embrace. She pushed her tongue into my mouth and we both breathed hard. Then she pulled away and snatched her book bag. "I can't do this, Garr. Please. I've got to go." She hurried across the bridge.

I thought about running after her, but I didn't. I picked up my books and turned back toward Collegetown. All right she loves me, and if not, she thinks about me all the time, I thought. She's engaged to a zillionaire, and he's wonderful and thoughtful. Is that what she has to decide? Gorvoy had said it was no contest; the zillionaire would win hands down. Gorvoy was never wrong.

For the next two months, Jenny avoided me. She'd talk to the cook, to Gorvoy, and to the waitresses, and then she'd disappear to eat later with the sisters. When she couldn't avoid me, she would say a polite hello and slip away. Once, Jenny was dining with the sisters and caught me watching her through the small diamond-shaped window on the kitchen door. She looked away but she had seen me. Then she got up and left the dining room.

THE CAMPUS ERUPTED that spring. Nixon had just moved

into the White House, and the war expanded even further although the President promised we'd be out of Vietnam in three years. Draft card burning became commonplace with staged demonstrations everywhere; the campus saw sit-ins and teach-ins and everything in-between. The drug scene grew from grass to speed to acid. Coeds took off their bras. The campus was fully divided.

I discarded the idea of going to grad school, thinking even if I did enroll, there was no guarantee of deferment. I had no prospects of marriage, I didn't want to claim to be a conscientious objector, expatriating to Canada seemed absurd, I didn't see much difference between the National Guard and the Army, and I didn't particularly want to design war machines.

Randy came up with a brilliant idea. By now the Selective Service had given him the 4-F for his claim as a homosexual. In the middle of the term, I had faked an excuse to get out of a prelim exam, complaining of a bad back. I had even gone to the campus clinic to obtain a medical excuse. I told Randy I had figured out a long time ago the doctors could never be certain of my claim—even X-rays could not confirm or disprove it. When I told him I'd been doing this to avoid deadlines since freshman year, he stood up.

"That's it, man," he said. "Look, the clinic will have four years of your back troubles documented with all kinds of possible diagnoses. All you've got to do is get a doctor from the clinic, or any doctor for that matter, to say that you've got unpredictable back problems. The army bureaucracy won't be able to take you."

I jumped up and yelled, "Far out!"

It was foolproof. I'd seen the stacks of manila folders of my back complaints. Possible diagnoses ranged from herniated disks to a small nerve canal to torn cartilage. And it wasn't difficult to find a doctor in the clinic who'd write a letter for me. The campus divide extended even to its doctors. I'd heard a Dr. Rosen was fiercely anti-war and helped guys get out of the draft. When I approached him, the good doctor was glad to fill a hefty box with my medical records, completely disheveled and unorganized, and send it to my draft board. He wrote a cover letter about my tenuous and unpredictable back. Dr. Rosen told me my case was strong, and that he had successfully appealed for others with fewer documents. My draft problem was solved.

The problem was I was still unhappy about Jenny. Unlike the draft situation which I had originally thought an impossible problem, things with Jenny were at a dead end. It was over. So I walked around the campus in misery. Gorvoy called me a schmuck.

In early April a takeover of the student union building by armed black students made national news. The students alleged the university and its judicial system were racist and that there was no progress in establishing a black studies program. Members of a fraternity tried to clash with the black students, and the Students for a Democratic Society formed a ring around the building in support of the takeover. State police from several cities across New York moved into town. A few days later, a negotiated settlement was reached, and the radical students were seen leaving the building, guns held high. If the campus had been divided before, the takeover split it like a gorge. I had two classes that morning. One professor walked in and said, "This is our school, and no one with guns is going to dictate terms to us. Class is dismissed for the semester." The other professor reacted differently. "If anyone needs a high grade to keep from flunking out, come and see me. I'll do what I can to stop Nixon."

I was in sympathy with the blacks. The few who were on campus weren't part of the community. They were there, but they were manifestly invisible. But did they really have to bring in guns? I didn't have the answer to that question, just as I didn't have the answer to all the turbulence in the country. And I didn't have any answer to my own turmoil with Jenny. That morning I saw an incident downtown that confused me even further. I spotted one of the black students who had been part of the takeover. His picture had been in every newspaper in the country. As he was getting out of his car, he noticed a cop eyeing at him. He faced the cop and gave a black power salute—raised arm with tightened fist. The cop stared at him, unperturbed. Then the radical student turned to the parking meter and inserted a nickel.

I wondered, was he a hypocrite? Hours ago, he and his companions illegally challenged the state troopers with rifles, and now, away from his friends and audience, he's Mr. Goody Two-Shoes and follows the rules to avoid a $2 ticket.

Or, was he a good citizen? He had experienced injustice and taken courageous action.

Gorvoy was out of town with the debate team in New York, and I was left to do the dishes. The cook had gone home, and the waitresses dropped off the dishes and left for a lawn party.

"Hello, Garr," I heard Jenny say. I was finishing the plates and my back was to the kitchen door, but I knew it was her.

A fluorescent light was humming loudly. "Hello, Jenny."

"I've been avoiding you, and maybe that wasn't right. But, I just didn't know what to do."

"It's all right. I understand."

"How have you been?" she asked as if I had terminal cancer.

I placed the last dish on the rack and began to rinse them. Some spray ricocheted onto her face. "Sorry," I said and handed her a towel.

"I'd like to talk to you. Please?"

She helped me close the kitchen, and we walked out of the house toward campus. It was warm that June evening, and Jenny wore a skirt and a blue T-shirt.

"How about Noyes Lodge?" she asked. "We can get coffee there."

Noyes Lodge was a student hangout on a lake which fed into the gorge, and it was packed with students and loud music. I suggested we take a walk around the lake.

The sun had just set, turning the sky a dull silver. The humid air was still. "God, this is beautiful," she said. "How come there's no one here?"

"It's like this all the time," I told her. "Right here on campus, and no one bothers with it. I come here year-round. It's quieter than the library."

The woods surrounded the lake, the tall trees blocking the campus noise. We walked in silence on the long trail next to the water's edge. Jenny stopped to sit on a large trunk of a fallen hemlock next to the path.

"Garr, I need to explain some things to you."

I sat next to her. A bull frog bellowed, searching for a mate. A wood thrush sang. I knew what was coming. She was about to tell me she was going to marry Bill, but before that she needed to square things with me. "You don't owe me any explanation," I said. You've already given me one. I think I'm supposed to hope you'll have a happy life. And I do, Jenny."

"I am going to marry Bill," she said. "I think you know I have deep feelings for you. And, I wanted to say goodbye to you, properly and face to face."

I continued to stare at the smooth water.

"Please look at me," she said.

I turned to her and there was enough light to see her wet eyes. She kissed me and her tears moved down her cheeks onto mine. Jenny stood up and looked down at me. Her eyes were fixed, and she lifted her T-shirt off and unhooked her brassiere. She breathed deeply and waited. I stood and brought her to me, her breasts pressing against me.

WE LAY STILL on a bed of dried leaves and humus. Neither of

us moved as our breathing slowed, our passion sucked away by the evening air. Jenny's body glimmered by the quarter moon. She sobbed quietly.

"Jenny."

She wiped her tears with her hand. "I'm very happy, Garr," she said. She stood and dressed quietly and then kissed me.

I wrapped my arm around her, and we walked along the trail, the moon's reflection shimmering between the trees. We said nothing and moved onto on to Thurston Avenue. Then she quickened her pace as if she were signaling me to let go of her arm. When I released her, she began to weep. She turned to me and said, "Good bye, Garr." She moved her head to my chest, hugged me, turned, and quickly walked beyond the streetlights into the darkness.

I could only stand and watch her leave me, unable to move. There was pain, rippling pain. And for what seemed like forever, I stared at the void she'd left. Anger crept in. If she loved me, why did she abandon me? If she didn't love me, why did she come to me? Was it money? Was that it? Money? And how had Gorvoy known what she would do?

I didn't sleep that night. I could only lie in bed and relive the day. I thought about Laura and saw the irony. I had been afraid to commit to Laura, I had abandoned her as Jenny had abandoned me. Except Jenny had left me because she was already committed. She was expected to marry, and soon. She would have security and money; it occurred to me maybe this was what the counterculture was rebelling against.

I never saw Jenny again. Later one of the sisters told me she had left town early after she finished her last exam, not bothering to wait for her diploma. And many Gamma sisters would attend her wedding in Connecticut. I continued to feel empty and relive the pain whenever I'd think of her. But as with Laura, the hurt diminished with time though her memories persisted.

BY THE CLOSING months of the year, an American had walked on the moon, the war in Vietnam had intensified even further, and the race riots continued. On a farm near a place called Woodstock in upstate New York, nearly half a million people partied at a three-day festival that became a symbol of the hippie movement.

In the last month of the decade, the government instituted the draft lottery, which determined one's eligibility for the draft by his birth date. Jeff and Kathy married that summer, and he was never called; I received my 4-F deferment; and Randy remained a 4-F homosexual. Randy's birth date, June 8th, was assigned a draft number 366. He would never have been called.

The so-called Sixties were just picking up steam.

About the Author

After receiving degrees from Cornell, Michael Ahn worked on the Apollo space program before moving on to teach and consult for business and government. This is his first book of fiction. He lives in a small town in California.

38694649R00117

Made in the USA
Charleston, SC
13 February 2015